Underneath the Moon 5

DAN HOLT
and
MAX HOLT

Published by:

MaxHoltMedia

DAN HOLT and MAX HOLT

OTHER SCI-FI BOOKS BY DAN HOLT
Underneath the Moon
Underneath the Moon 2
Underneath the Moon 3
Underneath the Moon 4, with Max Holt
Keepsake
Sleep Mode
(The above releases are also on Kindle and Audio, via Audible.com)
Intended future releases –
  Underneath The Moon 6

OTHER SCI-FI BOOKS BY MAX HOLT
Alien Planet
Series - AI Rising (Book One) THE DOME, with Dan Holt
Intended future releases –
  AI Rising (Book Two) ANDROID REBELLION

DAN HOLT and MAX HOLT

Disclaimer: This is a work of fiction. Names, characters, businesses, places, events, and incidents are either the products of the author's imagination or used in a fictitious manner. Except where permission has been granted, any resemblance to actual persons, living or dead, or actual events is purely coincidental.

Cover design by Max Holt Media, with Eddie Holt

ISBN: 13: 978-1-944537-31-9

Published by: Max Holt Media
303 Cascabel Place,
Mount Juliet, TN 37122
www.maxholtmedia.com
On facebook at www.facebook.com/maxholtmedia
        Email – max@maxholtmedia.com
        Twitter - @maxholtmedia

DAN HOLT and MAX HOLT

Spaceport Zeta, a floating beacon in deep space, has been discovered. It guards the Vortex; the entryway into the galaxy's vast wormhole system, enabling rapid travel to the innermost reaches of the Milky Way. Someone or **something** *inside has beckoned the giants and earth's 'little ones' to enter the unknown. Will the crew of the Omni-Star leave the safety of Zeta and risk everything to discover where they came from and* ***WHO THEY REALLY ARE?***

CONTENTS

DAN HOLT and MAX HOLT

Prologue

Alpha Centauri Star System
The planet Zannia

For days, following the strange transmission from the Object now in the Archives, life on Zannia came to a stand-still, as the giant and human populations anticipated some sort of immediate response from *somewhere*. When none came, life slowly returned to normal.

DAN HOLT and MAX HOLT

Chapter 1

QUANTUM

The strange space-object, stored in the Achieves, had activated and projected a hologram of the Quantum Communications Formula. The Object then went silent. Zannia's science team was now assembled in their lab in the sky to begin researching the formula's meaning and application.

The 30,000 miles-tall space-elevator, supporting their lab some 23,000 miles above the planet's surface, gave notice of its gentle swaying motion, only when it reversed its movement every few hours. It swayed a leisurely two miles backward and forward, at its midpoint, in line with the planet's orbital rotation. Each transit was majestically halted by the mathematically-correct ballast of the obliging counterweight. Such enormous tonnage of material had to be handled gently and respectfully. The team had gotten used to it. The elevator's tower held their research lab above Zannia's atmosphere and well into the fabric of space, the subject of their research.

Now, the golden fleece of the space age, how to apply the Quantum Communications Formula, was being sought-after with total dedication. To effectively interact with distant worlds, one must be able to communicate in a timely manner, within reason. To wait years, from transmission of a message to receiving an answer, completely canceled any practical trade or even simple community interaction. It was the first stumbling block upon reaching the capability to traverse the interstellar distances.

Zannian scientists had been tackling the issue for many years. The pursuit took on new enthusiasm upon the discovery of Quantum Entanglement; the realization that there are some atoms, separated by great distances but interlocked, or entangled, with each other. It could be described as *one atom matching the movement of the other,* instantly at any distance, whether it be an inch or a light-year (6 trillion miles); there would be no difference in the two. The secret was in the *fabric of space.* It was believed to be a, sort of, Cloud. Anything transmitted into it would be received everywhere instantly. It simply had to be retrieved with whatever electronic equipment or fields or energies, that were necessary. The question the scientists still hadn't answered was, what is the mechanism that locks atoms together or could enable galaxy-wide instant communications?

Eons earlier, upon the detection of emerging life on Zannia, two Modules, containing the secrets of the Quantum world, were buried on the planet to await discovery; which would be the tell-tale sign of the presence of sentient beings. When the Zannians had arisen into cognitive life, their mining operations had discovered one of the Modules. When they eventually abandoned the planet, they took it with them, still not knowing its significance, and stored it on Earth's moon.

When the Module was removed from the moon and was on the ship in open space, being returned to

Zannia, it signaled the mysterious Object, which was then dispatched. The Object first intercepted the two starships, in route from Earth to Zannia, and was reunited with the first Module.

When the Object arrived on Zannia, still missing one Module, it continued to search. When it had completed its mission and both Modules were assembled, the secret of Quantum Communications was revealed.

Now, the formula lay before the scientists. Their task was to determine what it meant. No one knew for sure who or *what* would receive that final signal Mentar had activated when he pushed the green button on the Object. It had sent out a powerful transmission and then had gone dark, and remained silent.

DAN HOLT and MAX HOLT

Chapter 2

SRE-17

Jack and Brenda Owenby, Co-Mayors of Little One City on Zannia, were busy managing the growing human colony. Several marriages had already been officiated and a few newborns were the delight of the whole colony, as well as the giants of Zannia.

In their daily interactions with Zannians, a general theory had surfaced, regarding the enormous size difference between the Zannians and the Earthers. Many felt, since Zannia was approximately the same size as the Earth, the likely cause was the food produced on the different planets. Here was a golden opportunity to run a definitive test of the theory. The starship Cosmos was parked on Zannia for a scientific study regarding the ecology, and was producing Earth food. The starship Little One was there as well, producing Zannian food. Of course, the nearby fields also provided Zannian cuisine. So, a timed test was arranged.

Brenda had taken on the task of coordinating the Food Test. Half the colony, including Brenda, would eat food grown on Zannia, while the other half, including Jack, remained on an Earth-food diet. The test would tell whether the Zannian food was the source of the growth experienced by the giants, since the gravity-well, spin, and atmosphere of both planets closely matched.

Designated shoppers of the two test groups had acquired all food from their respective 'supermarkets.' Those consuming Earth-food only, were at the impromptu shopping area just inside the spaceport. The 'store' was opened soon after the starship Cosmos had arrived from Earth. The greenhouse and hydroponics sections within the starship were never shut down. It was far too involved to get them up-and-running again to warrant a temporary shut-down. It supplied food and oxygen for the starship all the time. When in port, it would open a store and supply its bounty to the using public, wherever it was parked. The staff would prepare the food, through the canning process, and store as much as practical, then stock the store, a farmer's market of sorts, with the balance.

The giants' starship, Little One, did the same; cooking and preparing the food grown in Zannian fields. Hence, providing convenient supplies for the test group, eating Zannian food. Both test groups were eating vegetarian diets; the standard diet aboard a starship.

The test results of the experiment gradually began to reveal the truth. The chemistry of the host planet's soil determined the dwellers physical size, at least in the test subjects represented here. The first evidence was declared by Brenda Owenby. She, one morning, approaching Jack for the routine 'good morning' kiss, looked him in the eye: "Jack, you're shrinking," she said playfully.

He stopped and stared at Brenda for a long moment: "Oh, my God, Brenda; you *are* growing! It **is** the food!"

All the test-subjects were summoned to the conference room of Little One City, the Earth colony on Zannia, for the first very detailed, accurate, physical measurements. Everyone on Zannian food exclusively were an average of three-quarters of an inch taller than when they had arrived months earlier. A few, like Brenda, had grown just over an inch. It seemed conclusive. The chemical makeup of a planet, being present in its food, determined the size of the planet's inhabitants, within the allowances of the planets gravity-well. The colonists, in a unique and opportune setting, had stumbled onto a whole new area of scientific study.

Of course, the biggest question in the minds of the researchers was…Why? During their analysis of the soil on Zannia, they had catalogued the chemical make-up of the fields and gardens, identifying 17 primary chemical enzymes that were also present in the food grown there. When the 17th enzyme finally had its turn in the vacuum chamber, under the electron microscope, the Lab Tech did a double-take. He couldn't believe what he saw. He called over his giant counter-part to confirm his finding. When the giant turned from the viewing eyepiece, his bewildered look was mirrored on the tech's face. He opened a communications channel to the Chief Researcher and gave him the news.

Later, Colonel Jimmy Austin, Captain of the Cosmos, answered his phone.

"Colonel, this is Professor Jacobson, at the Food Test Lab. Mentar is on this call too. I need to see both of you at the Lab as soon as possible.

After a slight pause, Mentar, the giants' leader, asked, "Why, is there a problem?"

"No, sir, uh…well, maybe. It's more of a *finding*. You and the colonel can decide if it's a problem."

When the two leaders walked into the Lab, the entire test team was there, along with Jack and Brenda.

Professor Jacobson got straight to the point. "As you both know, the Food Test determined that our suspicions were true; that the primary factor in the sustained growth of the Zannian population and the humans eating Zannian food, is the food grown here.

You also know that we have been subjecting the soil to numerous tests to determine which of the 17 main enzymes is the cause. The tests were inconclusive until we did the electronic microscope scan inside the vacuum chamber. Those were all normal, until we tested Enzyme 17. It appears that Number 17 is the *specific* cause of the growth in Zannians, and now in the human test subjects. Brenda is one of those subjects." Professor Jacobson paused a moment.

Mentar spoke: "Is there a problem with this enzyme other that the fact that it initiates growth?"

"Yes, sir. All tested enzymes were normal biologics except 17. We couldn't believe its makeup, so we tested it in the chamber three times. Number 17 is not a biologic...it is, uh...a synthetic."

Jimmy and Mentar stared at each other and back at the professor. Jimmy leaned forward. "Wait a minute! Are you saying that the enzyme is manmade... uh, giant made?"

"No sir; it was planted on Zannia in the beginning, probably before the planet was populated at all."

Mentar stared for a moment. "So, someone else seeded Zannia with this, uh, chemical to make sure we would grow to our current size?"

The professor nodded. "Exactly. Probably some kind of sophisticated test to see how much you would grow. But, it is not really a chemical...it's more of a bio-mechanical enzyme. Our designation is SRE-17...Self-Replicating Enzyme number 17. "

"What do you mean, *self-replicating*?"

"It reproduces itself, much like a normal living cell, but it is part biological and part mechanical...more specifically...electronic. It is so microscopic we have not been able to analyze it internally, but we surmise that there is a nano-level processor inside that ensures the enzyme's survival, regardless of its surroundings. We have yet to determine where it gets its power. That's the biggest question, since these things have been reproducing for well over 100,000 years. The parts-per-billion measurement of the enzyme in the soil remained the same, no matter where we collected the samples on the planet. Whatever this is, it has the technology to control its own growth, so as not to over-populate the soil."

Mentar and Jimmy were speechless for more than a few moments. Finally, Mentar said, "But, Zannians abandoned the planet about 100,000 Earth-years ago. Why did our species continue growing to our current size after we left Zannia?"

The professor's giant counter-part spoke up. "Sir, historical archives recovered from our former facilities on Earth's moon show that those who abandoned Zannia took soil to establish the hydroponic and greenhouse operations on the ships. Over the generations of Solaris Four's population, the enzyme replicated itself to permeate the soil there and on the other planets that were populated, except Earth…they never populated Earth. The gardens that sustained our retiree population on the moon were all contained in separate growth-pots."

Jimmy nodded. "Right; I read that on your first journey back to Zannia, you took all of the growth-pots from the Moon to use on your ship."

The professor continued the thought. "That would mean that the enzyme does not exist in Earth's soil. If that is true, the colony of giants currently on Earth do not have the advantage of SRE-17." He looked up at Mentar. "The giants on Earth, meaning any future offspring, may not follow your historical growth pattern. They could…uh…"

Mentar interrupted. "You mean, they could end up human size?"

"Maybe. We need to get a message to Earth so the scientists there can confirm the absence of SRE-17 and begin to monitor the colony population for growth...or lack thereof. When Cosmos returns to Earth, Colonel Austin can deliver the message."

Finally, Jack entered the conversation. "What about our colony? We can't stay on Earth-food forever. Cosmos is producing it, but the ship will return to Earth soon. Then, we will all be eating Zannian food. Does that mean we will all end up being 40 feet tall? Instead of staying *humans,* will we become *humannians*?"

The professor held up his hands. "Wait; before we go off the deep end with questions, we have already formed a study group to address those concerns. Since giant and human DNA and metabolisms are somewhat different, the growth changes here, and in the colony on Earth may not be as drastic as we imagine. Give us some time to look at the possibilities and assess the impact.

"Better still," Mentar began, "develop an additive for our soil that will seek out this enzyme and neutralize it. Make it aggressive enough that we can introduce it around the planet and it will get rid of it forever."

Everyone was staring at Mentar. Mentar's jaw was set. "I don't like my size being determined by something artificial or synthetic. I was relieved to discover that we didn't make...uh, create the little ones; that, instead, we both came from the same cradle. It just may be that we are supposed to be the same size."

The professor nodded. "Over the centuries, the people of Earth have gradually gotten taller. Mentar, you just may be right."

Mentar and Jimmy both looked at the professor.

He continued. "We will attempt do that. I'm surprised that you would make that request but, somehow, I like it. We'll get right on it."

"Call me when it's ready. Jimmy and I will have a ceremony when we introduce the first seeding. Then, perhaps, one day, our descendants can look each other in the eye."

Chapter 3

THE WADDELL CONE

In light of the discovery of the Object and its magical and mysterious message, Mentar, Zannia's President, assigned a group of the miners to explore the newly opened maze of tunnels for any more possible objects. There were several tunnels they had not yet checked. Some of them required the miners to enlarge the access points from one tunnel to the other, for admittance. With miles of tunnels to be investigated, the vigil became a daily routine.

Mentar and Jimmy paid a visit to the lab in the sky.

"Anything, yet?" Mentar inquired.

The chief scientist poised his fingertips on each other, and then turned toward Mentar. "This formula is very, very complicated. However, we have discovered the value **1.008** embedded inside this formula in several places."

"1.008; what does that mean?"

"It's the atomic weight of hydrogen. We don't know why it's there or what it means...yet. Hydrogen makes up 75% of the galaxy. Even in deep space, completely empty space, raw space, there's at least one hydrogen atom in each cubic yard by volume. Hydrogen is everywhere."

"Well, keep at it. That's a start. That formula is very important to us. Someone planted those Modules here on Zannia, who knows when, for us to find. There has to be a very significant reason for us to discover how to access Quantum Communications."

Jimmy nodded. "Yes, I think *someone, somewhere,* wants to talk to us."

Upon their return to the surface, they were summoned by the miners. They had found something several miles into the tunnel system. The miners had arranged a harness and were on their way out of the mountain with a different kind of object. Mentar and Jimmy were waiting by at the entrance. Two hours later, the group of miners came out of the tunnel carrying a Moai statue.

"Oh, my God," Jimmy said, "what's that doing here?!"

Mentar stared at the statue for a long moment. "The Moai on Easter Island were copies made by the Elders, who were rescued from the sea. The one on the moon was originally found on Zannia and had been brought along when our ancestors abandoned the planet thousands of years ago. It, and now this one, were placed here by someone. Were they leaving a trail for us to follow? What are they trying to tell us? Think about this, Colonel, they were carved after our likeness."

"Or," Jimmy said slowly, holding Mentar's eyes, "the other way around. Perhaps you, your race, all your kind, were genetically engineered in the likeness of the Moai."

Deep in the halls of the spaceport was Zannia's ground-based research lab. When the Elders, having been dug out of their sub-ocean sleep on Earth, were returned to Zannia, they soon found it. It was almost as if they could sense it. A small group found it to be home, their place to be every day, always searching for the new and unknown.

While the 'lab in the sky' was getting all the attention and fanfare, this small, dedicated group was digging into getting more speed capability for Little One and Cosmos, their two main interstellar ships, to further lower the transit time, star-system to star-system. The answer came, almost as a gift from the universe to the Elders, for spending 500 centuries in a watery tomb, quietly waiting, quietly trusting, until the shovels and ships came for them.

In their lab, the scientists soon made an amazing discovery that would change space flight forever. They named it after the navy admiral, Irwin Waddell, who had managed their recovery at Easter Island; the long climb back to life. It would be forever known as: **The Waddell Cone**.

The effect created by The Waddell Cone turned out to be simpler than the scientists expected. They wondered how they had *missed it* for so many thousands of years. They explained it like this: On both starships, three massive generators were mounted on its perimeter, inside the upper deck, at 120-degree increments. One was dead center, aft on the vessel, and the other two were installed at each side of the massive windshield. These two were designed to shield the starship during acceleration. Three additional generators would be mounted in the same fashion in the engine room, to shield the ship during deceleration. The generators would project beams forward for a half-million miles ahead of the ship to coalesce and form a magnetic 'bow,' a field that would simply spread space apart, with all its contents, and allow the ship to pass through. Then space would 'splash' back together, actually leaving a wake to slowly dissipate.

The scientists were beaming with accomplishment. Jimmy could have sworn that their noses looked bigger. Transit time, Zannia to Earth, would now be reduced from eight years to two years and three months.

The ship would not actually exceed the speed of light. The Waddell Cone would open space, creating something similar to a small wormhole, allowing the ship to simply skip, or slip through, the fabric of space.

There was a downside, a payment, for this gift of much greater speed. Once the Waddell Cone was engaged, no excursion craft of any kind could be allowed to leave the mothership. The Cone around the ship was large enough for a shuttlecraft, but If an excursion craft accidentally wandered outside the Cone, it would be instantly vaporized by unmeasurable friction. The crew couldn't take that chance. So, upon engaging the Waddell Cone, all exits of the ship would be automatically sealed. If an emergency occurred and the Waddell Cone had to be disengaged, the ship would automatically revert back to the eight-year transit velocity; a phenomenon undetectable inside the vessel, except through instrument readings that would alert the crew.

"We've made it to the stars," Jimmy whispered.

DAN HOLT and MAX HOLT

Chapter 4

THE REPORT

The scientists who came to study Zannia were hard at work to finish their analysis. Earth's starship, Cosmos, moored at Kaavar's spaceport on the planet Zannia, still waited for them to complete their assignments. The calendar-year's investigation into the cause of Zannia's near death, and her miraculous come-back to a plush, rich, bountiful planet, had been very detailed. This investigation was deemed critical to Earth's well-being in the future. When it was complete, Cosmos would set sail for home.

The Earth Scientists

The team of scientists from Earth, all 96 of them, gathered in the conference room of the spaceport. Cosmos' crew, Zannia's dignitaries, and the colonists were all invited to hear the report amassed by the researchers. All were handed a copy for reference. It read:

THE FINDINGS OF THE RESEARCH TEAM ON ZANNIA'S ECOLOGICAL FAILURE AND RECOVERY

DAN HOLT and MAX HOLT

By

Alfred Tennenbaum – Chief Scientist

Systematic excavations at multiple sites around the planet during the past year to study the strata, including studies up to a mile underground, the access provided by the base anchoring system of the space elevator, has revealed that the cause of Zannia's ecological downturn was two celestial events.

In the past, Zannia had one sun and a moon. Based on the similarities of the strata, it is our opinion that the system, about a quarter million years ago, was virtually identical to our Earth/Moon system. Based on our studies and the present configuration of this system, we believe we can piece together how the Zannian system was changed.

A rouge star, probably Zannia 2, accompanied by a large planet, perhaps a gas giant, passed by Zannia's moon, with the gas giant planet coming very close, at a high velocity. It pulled Zannia's moon free from its orbit, giving it escape velocity. The rouge star, or sun, being slowed by the moon's and Zannia's gravity, settled into orbit around Zannia 1. The two suns of Alpha Centauri, Zannia 1 and Zannia 2, began a new celestial dance, orbiting each other. The planet Zannia, enduring all these foreign gravitational tugs, settled into its present orbit around the center of mass of the two suns.

If there were Zannians on the planet at that time, and they survived the shake-up, they would have surely been knocked back to their stone age. Those events set Zannia on a course to oblivion. Nature had to build a new ecological system based on the new mechanics of the star system. The recovery of the planet was initiated by the vacating of it by the Zannians. The Zannians had caused the extinction of the predatory animals, and then, by vacating, allowed nature to recover and the planet to become healthy again.

One other thing. As you know, recently, a Moai was discovered buried here on Zannia, a find with very subtle implications. A Moai was also discovered to have been planted on Earth's moon, and, of course, there are the copies on the Earth, on Easter Island. This is rather bold, but it's our opinion that Zannia's lost moon is now Earth's found moon. When ripped from this star system, it wandered the galaxy until Earth captured it. What an amazing development and the wildest of coincidences.

There may be a natural gravitational corridor from Alpha Centauri to our Solar System, provided by the mechanics of the layout of the Milky Way Galaxy. This gravitational influence could be caused by the location of the galactic core, the location of the Sagittarius Spiral Arm, and the Orion Spur. The Solar System is located between the two spiral arms. Whatever the influence, that is keeping the stars grouped into spiral arms, may have gently nudged the moon to its new home. If this theory is true, the moon would have been coached in the direction of the Solar System until another influence took over—Earth. Much more study needs done by the colonists here and Earth's scientists back home. The statues are the key to our conclusion. What's the origin of the Moai? When and where and why were they created? We have a starship; let's find out. To quote one of our earlier scientists: "Somewhere, something incredible is waiting to be known"

END REPORT

The research scientists began to understand the natural processes that saved a planet from its downward spiral, caused by the celestial upheaval. It was a symbiotic secret, yet, right out in the open. The animal herds and their natural cycle were the keys. As the herds began to rebuild their numbers, no longer at the bottom of a ravenous food chain, and roam the planet, their natural cycle of ingesting the grasses and other plants, then their excretions in such numbers, revitalized and enriched the land, producing more prolific growth of the grasses, plants, and trees.

Though more study was needed, many of the scientists were ready to go home. The portable world of starship Cosmos beckoned. A few of the colonists had also voiced a desire to be on Cosmos when she headed for Earth. Zannia was okay, however, it just wasn't home. They had voiced their feelings and had moved back aboard Cosmos, a little piece of home parked on Zannia for a few more days. Then, Cosmos would head for the flat plains of Kansas, with its occasional dust storms, Earth smells, one sun, and home.

Cosmos Conference Room

Jeremy Weston, age 17, about to mark the completed year as an apprentice on rotor pod technology, recalled his escapades to the engine room during Cosmos' journey from Earth to Zannia. His mouth watered thinking about his apprehension near the rotor pods, eating the 'borrowed' tomato from hydroponics. It accented his love of being among the rotor pods, with their sleek design and appearance and their distinctive hum while they were delivering power for the ship.

Now, he was close to becoming a bonafied technician. He had applied and was approved to take care of the rotor-pod-enabled ships that would remain on Zannia for use by the colonists. His mentor and trainer, Chief Matthew Dolan, would be returning to Earth with Cosmos. There was no way Colonel Austin would part with his engine room expert. So, it was important that Jeremy be capable, learned, and dedicated to the maintenance of the rotor pods remaining on Zannia. After all, they had taken humans to the stars.

Today, in the conference room of Cosmos, with Colonel Austin, his bridge crew, and the technical staff of Cosmos' engine room present, Jeremy Weston was being awarded his certification. After citing the areas of training that Jeremy had completed, the Chief presented him his plaque containing the official document. The applause lasted minutes. Then, the Chief nodded to an assistant. He came forward with a platter with a domed metal cover over it. It had a single knob in the top center.

"Jeremy Weston," the Chief began, "the day you first came to the engine room of Cosmos and visited with us at the age of 8, you left something."

The assistant lifted the cover from the platter. Underneath, was the salt shaker he had used when he was eight years old... and a fresh tomato.

Chapter 5

THE ZOLAADINE MAN

Zannia's Spaceport's Control Tower

The shift leader in the spaceport control tower watched the shuttle lift off with the day-shift crew of radio astronomers on board. It routinely departed every morning, delivering the day-shift to the facilities and picking up the night-shift and returning them to the spaceport. When it disappeared into the distance, he began scanning the horizon around the control tower; a routine habit. A hundred and eighty degrees around the horizon, he spotted a column of smoke spiraling toward the sky. He grabbed a pair of binoculars, pointed them at the far-away column, and adjusted the focus.

"Fire!" he shouted. "There's a forest fire in the west, close to the horizon. Dispatch a shuttle immediately and get a visual."

He keyed the radio to Mentar. The government leader responded immediately. "Go ahead, Tower."

"Mentar, we have a forest fire at the horizon in the west, about thirty miles away."

"What happened? How did it start?"

"We don't know yet; we've dispatched a shuttle for a closer look. We'll have a visual in about ten minutes."

"Call me when you have that."

Mentar closed the link, then called Colonel Austin. Cosmos' commander was aboard Cosmos going over the preparations for departure to Earth. "Colonel, I just got notice from the control tower. We have a forest fire on the western horizon. A shuttle is on the way for a visual."

"Oh, my God, Mentar, this plush jungle will be an inferno! Any threat to your infrastructure?"

"We'll know shortly."

"We can help extinguish it if you need us. We've got six of our cargo shuttles, the guppies, on board. Each cargo hold will transport about 14,000 cubic feet of water."

"How do you fill the hold?"

"The ships are sealed. The rotors are in a vacuum. The crew cabin and cargo hold are both airtight, and independent of each other. We simply seal the crew cabin, submerse the ship in the ocean or a lake with the cargo hold open and allow it to fill, then close and seal the doors, fly to the fire, and dump it where it's needed."

"Colonel...like one of you *little ones* would say, that...is...smooth."

"Yeah, it works. We..."

"I'm getting a call from the spaceport tower." Mentar closed the link and opened the link to the tower.

"Mentar, we have a visual," came over the radio, "it looks like a meteor strike, a small one, ignited the fire; we have a thirty-foot crater. The fire's raging and there's a southerly wind fanning the flames toward the farms. They're about 50 miles north of the fire. We've got to get it under control right away."

"Okay," Mentar said. "Start moving some heavy equipment to the area to cut a fire break."

Mentar radioed Jimmy again. "Colonel, we will need those guppies. We have a southerly wind that is fanning the fire. It's moving toward the farms to the north. We are moving heavy equipment to the area to clear a fire break, just in case."

"I'll dispatch all the guppies. They'll need to know where the nearest body of water is. It will need to be at least thirty feet deep."

Jimmy thought about the two DOEs; the two specially equipped shuttles, heavily armed for defense, designated as *Defenders of Earth.* They each were equipped with twin laser cannons. They could cut a fire break very quickly.

"Mentar," Jimmy said. "I will have the two DOE's laser cut the trees along the fire break. They can do it quickly, then your equipment can clear the felled trees. I'll have a guppy full of water accompany them, in case the lasers ignite some of the foliage."

Captains Snyder and Abbott, pilots of the two DOEs, entered their respective machines and prepared to exit Cosmos and fly to the area under siege by fire. One guppy fired up to accompany them. Captain Snyder pulled out his log book and made an entry. He reflected on it momentarily. "I've got some unusual entries here since we were assigned to Cosmos."

"Yeah, me too," Abbott said. "This has got to be a first."

They exited the hangar bay and headed west. In a few minutes, they were over the area. Colonel Austin came on the radio. "Snyder, Abbot, to your right, you'll see Mentar's shuttle. Start there and cut a swath five-hundred-feet wide from that point toward the east. It will need to be about five miles long. Cut only the trees one-foot across and larger. Their equipment can get the rest. The guppy will handle any small fires you start with the lasers."

"Will do," Snyder said and began the process. The lasers went through the tree trunks instantly. It was a constant felling of trees as they progressed eastward. It looked like a scene out of the ancient Star Wars movies. When the bulldozers showed up, they began pushing the felled trees north to the edge of the firebreak.

The remaining guppies from Cosmos were right behind the DOEs, ready to attack the fire. They immediately headed south toward the mountains, as per Mentar's instructions. Ten miles away, they spotted the highland lake. It was fed by a waterfall from the highlands and had a river exiting toward the ocean. They flew to the body of water, descended to the surface, then with the cargo bays open, slowly submerged, allowing the bays to fill with water. Each guppy then closed the cargo bay door, sealing the bay full of water, about 80,000 gallons of it. Then, they rose out of the lake and headed for the burning forest. In a line, they flew over the fire and opened the bay doors. Immediately, most of the water was turned to steam when it was released and fell into the inferno. The dampening effect was very little.

Colonel Austin, observing the operation, keyed his radio. "Guppies, fly ahead of the fire about a hundred yards and soak the forest with water to slow down the fire. Watch you hull temperatures."

The guppies flew in line, circling to the lake and the fire, dumping thousands of gallons of water on the undergrowth. The water formed multiple ponds and puddles, saturating the foliage with water. When the fire reached the soaked timber and brush, it slowed dramatically. The guppies were there with bay after bay of water to dump on the flames. Gradually, the flames were brought under control. The fire reached the firebreak in a few places and then was extinguished.

Mentar called the spaceport. "Set up a patrol of this area, for a couple of days, to guard against any re-igniting embers."

Two shuttles were assigned surveillance of the stricken area. They would overfly it every two hours until all were satisfied there was no further danger.

The miles-square aftermath of the forest fire

Zannian scientists and members of the colonists were examining the parched area left behind by the fire. Mentar, Kronos, and Jimmy were touring the scene.

The scientists were busy about their own various interests. Some were interested in the soil condition after burn-off, a methodology used by some to enrich depleted soil on some farms. Others were viewing what had to be done for re-planting and then wanted records of the productivity of the land after being relieved of it underbrush and multiple saplings and off-shoots of the previous heavy growth.

And, there were those that simply wanted to explore this area of the planet, as it was the first time that eyes had fallen on this part since the Zannians returned. This particular area had not been visited before and no one knew if there were any surprises there. As fate would have it, there was a reward for the curious.

A team of six explorers was pulling at a pile of burned-out timbers with soil-handling tools when they exposed a dome-shaped *something,* buried underground. The crown of the rounded metal object was about the size of basketball. Curiosity had them digging out around it. Down about a foot or so, they exposed a pair of eyes. They were clear glass, obviously artificial.

Amenvaar, the team leader, stepped back, looking at the exposed head-like find. "It's a robot!" he said, and then turned to a team member. "Go get Mentar!"

The team was vigorously digging around the figure, exposing the shoulders. They were about four feet wide. Mentar's pilot landed his ship nearby and he and his colleagues approached the robot. They walked all the way around it. Mentar looked at Amenvaar,

"Looks like your team has found a robot, or an automaton. Any movement or reaction?"

"No. It's seems to be completely dead. No power at all."

"Okay, go ahead and dig it out. We'll take it to the spaceport and examine it. Also, let's get someone out here to check the strata when you have it out and see how long it's been buried here. Based on the size of the cranium, if he's properly proportioned, he's going to be about fifteen to twenty feet tall."

"Acknowledged. We'll be careful not to damage it."

The Spaceport Lounge

Mentar, Jimmy, and Kronos, Mentar's Assistant, had returned to the spaceport for lunch. They were expounding theories on what the newly discovered robot could be about; who had brought it here and was it part of the original society, the ones who eventually abandoned Zannia for survival.

Mentar changed the subject. A man, one of the Elders, had come to his office and asked for a private meeting. A meeting Mentar subsequently arranged.

41

He turned to Colonel Austin. "Jimmy," he said and paused.

Colonel Austin looked up. Mentar had used his first name; unusual for Zannia's leader. Mentar continued: "Ah, Colonel, one of my people, Kaabar, came to my office the other day. He asked to meet with me in private. I honored the request. This man is 118 years old. He's still in reasonable health. He requested to return to Earth with you and join the colonists there. His grandson was among the students that perished in the secondary tunnel on the moon. Before life is over for him, he wants to visit the memorial again. Then, Colonel, when his time comes, he wants to join his grandson on the moon."

Colonel Austin was quiet for a moment. "Tell him we would be glad to have him aboard. I will personally see that he gets to the moon and to the dedication site for his grandson. And, I'll see to his final request."

"Should he succumb before you arrive on earth…"

"We will prepare him and see that he's entombed with his grandson."

"Thank you…I'll share the news with him."

The Excavation Site

Amenvaar's shovel appeared to have penetrated the robot's right leg. Puzzled, the team quickly dug out around it and cleared the loose soil. The right leg was missing from the robot. At the break, the metal exterior appeared to have partially melted and then cooled, misshapen.

"A laser hit!" Amenvaar said. "Let's finish digging it out and then see if we can find the missing leg. The team began digging with a new vigor. Amenvaar opened his communicator and called Mentar.

Mentar closed his communicator and turned to Jimmy. "Colonel, that was Amenvaar. The robot they are excavating was hit by laser fire, severing one of its legs."

"Oh, really!"

"Let's go back out there and look around."

Mentar's shuttle touched down again at the site. The crew had the robot out of the hole and lying on its back. It looked about fifteen feet tall. Its severed right leg was lying on the ground beside it. It did not seem to be of the highest technology. There were linkages sticking out of the hollow leg casing. The malformed leg reflected the damaged caused by the extreme heat of extended laser fire.

"Where did you find the leg?" Mentar said.

"It was in the bottom of the hole."

"So," Mentar commented, "he was deliberately placed here. He didn't just come to rest here and the ground grow over him through the millenniums."

"Notice the hands," Jimmy said, "they are patterned after the standard humanoid hand."

Mentar glanced at them and then at the head. The facial features were very human-looking, except for the ears. They were simply a round port with a recessed diaphragm.

"We've got to find out how long this guy has been buried here," Mentar observed. "I wonder if he was a warrior, a fighter, or was this simply an experiment and the thing went rogue and they had to take it down. Remember the automaton we had to destroy on Mars."

"Why would they leave it out here?" Kronos offered. "That doesn't make sense."

"That would indicate, if he's a warrior, that there was a war here on Zannia in the past. Dating this excavation is really important. Was this done before or after the Zannians left the planet? It may even date back to when the Module or the Moai was left here."

"That brings up a thought," Jimmy said. "When they have dated this site, have them go back into the tunnel system and date the site where they found the Moai."

"Good idea."

Three days later – Spaceport Conference Room

The Zannian scientist cleaned his glasses and put them back on. "Zolaadine Man," he began, "that's the name we've given our artificial friend. He has been standing in his grave for a very long time. He's constructed of Zolaadine metal, very tough, and an alloy we have yet to identify. There is no record of the other metal on Zannia. He was most likely placed there when Zannia had only one sun, and a moon. We checked his servo-mechanisms and he was not capable of locomotion, once his leg was severed. Therefore, he was deliberately placed in the position in which he was found. At the time it was done, the ground in that area was probably barren. We are looking at over a quarter-million years ago. A note: this study corroborates the conclusion reached by the Earth scientists, regarding Zannia's ecology and the dramatic celestial events that caused the catastrophic changes.

"We will be doing a detailed study of Zolaadine Man. Perhaps it will produce some insight into what the civilization that he belonged to was like. Further, we will test-dig around the excavation site for any other finds."

"Well," Mentar said. "It looks like we have a mystery. Perhaps, as time goes on, we will find more evidence and unravel it.

DAN HOLT and MAX HOLT

Chapter 6

THE VISITORS

Peak Island, Zannia

Life on Peak Island welcomed the new day. This day began with the unfolding of a mystery. The observatory on the island, during the night, had discovered a moving object that was completely out of step with the celestial dance of the thousands of stars that crossed the sky nightly. At first, it was believed to be another comet or asteroid; a stray piece of space debris. However, there was an issue. It had made a course change; one that would bring it to Zannia.

A radio telescope was quickly turned and locked onto it to see what could be *heard* from the object. The answer was quick to come. If it was a craft, but it was not transmitting. The staff keyed the communication radio to Mentar.

Mentar, sleeping in his private chamber, was awakened by the incessant buzz of his radio. He sat up, rubbed his face, and looked at his communicator; 5:30 a.m. He reached over and keyed the system and responded.

"Mentar, this is the Peak Island Observatory, there's an object approaching Zannia."

"An object?"

"Yes, sir. It's approaching from the Northeast."

"Space debris?"

"That's what we thought at first. We tracked it for two hours, then it made a course change."

"Course change!" Mentar said. "Are you sure?"

"Yes, sir. A course change that has it coming right for us. It is also slowing its speed. We have the radio telescope on it as well."

"Can you estimate its size?"

"Roughly, it's about a quarter-mile across."

Mentar became silent for a few moments then keyed the radio again. "How fast is it going?"

"It has slowed to just under 30,000 miles per hour."

"That's slow enough for braking and an approach."

"Yes, sir. We picked it up on the long-range scan. We didn't catch it early enough to determine where it came from. We are still checking on that."

"How long until it arrives?"

"At current velocity, it will arrive in eighty-one-point-six hours. Just over three days."

"Okay, stay on it," Mentar said. "I'll get back to you."

"Yes, sir. Zannia 'A' will be rising in an hour. We will lose visual, but we've got radio tracking on it. We'll pick it up visually again tonight."

"Good. Notify Parliament and the team at Spaceport."

Colonel Austin and his bridge crew were up and having coffee on the treetop landing pad of Little One City when his communicator sounded. The colonel keyed it and answered.

"Colonel," Mentar said, "we have an alien craft approaching Zannia from the Northeast."

"My, God!" Jimmy said, sitting straight up in his chair.

"I was just notified," Mentar added. It will arrive in about three days."

"Do they know where it came from?"

"Not yet. It is still over 2 million miles out. They estimate that the ship is about a quarter-mile in diameter. They're working on projecting where it came from. It made a course change a couple of hours after they spotted it, a course change which put it on trajectory for Zannia. I'll pick you up on my way to the spaceport."

Colonel Austin paged Captain Snyder's communicator: "Captain, where are you?"

"Cosmos' aft lounge, sir."

"We've just learned that a spacecraft of some type is approaching Zannia. It's three days away. Presently, we don't know anything about it except its relative size; about a quarter-mile in diameter. Meet us at the spaceport's main building right away.

"Yes, sir, on our way."

Captain's Snyder and Abbott looked at each other for a moment. "Seems orchestrated, doesn't it," Snyder said.

"I don't know about that," Abbott responded. "We have been here almost a year. There may be a million planets out there, just entering the beginnings of space travel, reaching out into the galaxy trying to make sense of it. You know, *why is all of this here; why is all of it so far apart?* The noise that our listening devices hear, background noise, may be those million voices all sounding together: *Who are we; where did we come from; why are we here?*" Abbott paused. "We may be the only ones who know those answers."

"Captain Abbott, you are a philosopher."

Bayan, Mentar, and Kronos, along with the Speaker and Deputy Speaker of Parliament touched down on the landing pad of Little One Village in Mentar's brand new personal shuttle and opened the outer doors. Colonel Austin, his bridge crew, and Jack Owenby, the appointed spokesman for the colonists, boarded the vessel. It lifted off and flew the two miles to the spaceport and descended to the pad in front of the main building. The crews of the two DOEs were standing out front of the entrance.

The group exited the shuttle, joined the crews waiting, entered the building, and were escorted to the meeting room. They saw the specially designed two-level meeting tables. Colonel Austin looked up at Mentar. "You plan ahead."

"Kronos thinks on his feet." Mentar responded, smiling.

Seated at the meeting tables, Mentar began: "Peak Island, last night, picked up an object moving across the sky. At first it was thought to be an asteroid or comet just over a thousand feet in diameter. But then, it made a course change; a course change that put it on a trajectory that will bring it to Zannia. If it continues on its present course and speed it will arrive in Zannian space in three days."

"Have they been able to plot a course on where it came from?" Melvin Faulkner, Cosmos telemetry officer, asked.

"Yes," Mentar said. Peak Island sent me a data message a few minutes ago. Based on tracking prior to the course change, it appears to have been launched from Zylon. On your charts, that's Bernard's Star. Zylon is roughly six light-years from Zannia and about that from Earth. The three-star systems; Earth's Sun, Zannia 'A' and 'B', and Zylon form a triangle. Tracing the unknown's path backwards, Zylon, or Bernard's Star, is the closest star on its path.

What do we do?" the Speaker asked.

"We find out who they are," Mentar responded. "We meet them when they enter Zannian space, hopefully with a welcome."

"I agree with you, Mentar, you should welcome them," Colonel Austin added. "However, we should not be sitting ducks."

"Sitting ducks?" Kronos responded.

"Completely vulnerable; it's an Earth expression. I recommend preparedness by stationing one of the DOEs over the spaceport and having the other accompany us to the projected point of arrival to welcome the unknown."

"Agreed," Mentar said.

Again, Mentar's communicator sounded. Noting the call was from Peak Island, he put it on speaker. "Go ahead Peak Island. We are in a meeting and I have you on speaker."

"Mentar, the incoming ship is decelerating further. The numbers have changed. Arrival, now, will be a little over four days. Precisely 108 hours, 26 minutes. Also, the velocity upon arrival will be correct for a geosynchronous orbit insertion above Zannia."

"That's a very accurate approach to this planet," Mentar offered. "It indicates that someone aboard ordered the numbers for the approach or there's very sophisticated automatic equipment aboard, steering the vessel." Mentar paused a moment. "Our spacelab, mounted on the tower of the space elevator, is at that altitude."

"Yes, sir. It's in no danger though. If the craft's approach stays the same, it will enter orbit over a thousand miles east of the spacelab; over raw jungle. It will be ahead of the spacelab and tower in the orbit. Because of its entrance angle it will oscillate north and south of the equator while remaining in sync with Zannia's rotation, unless it corrects for that angle. That's because its orbit will be a few degrees off the standard equatorial orbit for geosynchronous satellites."

"Thank you, Peak Island. Keep us informed."

Colonel Austin looked up at Mentar. "Shall we take the shuttles up to the insertion point and meet the craft? We can examine it. We can leave Captain Abbott here to protect the spaceport should it be threatened. We are dealing with an unknown here. Captain Snyder can accompany us to meet the alien ship."

The giants conversed in Moon language for a few moments, and then nodded in agreement. Mentar nodded to Colonel Austin and noted: "Let's assume this will be a peaceful encounter."

"Of course," Colonel Austin said. "I doubt if someone would travel six light-years to start a shooting war."

"Only in the movies," Abbot said.

DAN HOLT and MAX HOLT

Chapter 7

THE ENCOUNTER

The shuttles and DOEs were prepped for a rendezvous with the approaching Visitor. The evening of day three, some 22 hours before the expected arrival of the vessel, the two shuttles and two DOEs rose to 5000 feet and held. Captain Abbot, DOE 2, assumed a stationary position over the spaceport. Captain Snyder, DOE 1, remained in formation with the shuttles. They pressurized their crafts and began the climb to the geostationary insertion point, of the incoming alien ship, two thousand miles over the horizon and 23,000 miles up. Mentar and Jimmy were sure that such an advanced craft would be able to detect the presence of their ships, waiting above the planet. And, would just as surely consider it a prudent reaction to their approach to Zannia.

Captain Abbott watched the ships fly away toward the east, then looked around at the sprawling spaceport below. It was carved neatly out of the plush jungle. "What did they do with all those millions of board-feet of lumber?" he mused. Then he thought about the thousands of dwellings constructed in the saucer-shaped structures atop the many pedestals of the cities and way-stations around the planet. From his vantage point his eyes went across the canopy of the jungle, miles in all directions. The jungles were crawling alive with many different species of animals, benign, almost domesticated. A unique balance of nature that was forcibly altered by the giants, then abandoned. Nature stepped in and brought it back to balance and health.

Abbott's gunner broke the silence. "We are on an alien planet; hovering over an alien spaceport; protecting it from an incoming alien."

The three crewmembers looked at Sergeant Merle Winston, weapons expert, turned DOE gunner.

"Just sayin'," he grinned.

The welcoming armada arrived at the insertion point, rotated their ships toward the northeast and came to a hover, setting the ships' controls in the Station-Keeping mode. Mentar keyed the radio. "Peak Island, what's the latest?"

"Fifty-one minutes, sir. You should see them any minute almost directly overhead. Zannia and the Visitor will meet where you are in less than an hour. The craft is now at orbital insertion velocity."

Moments went by. "I see it!" Captain Snyder said. "It's black. That's odd for a ship designed to operate in raw sunlight."

"Ninety-nine percent of its journey is in starlight," Lt James West, Snyder's co-pilot, noted.

The three crews watched in anticipation as the alien craft loomed larger and larger. It adjusted its plane to be perpendicular to the pull of gravity, then smoothed out in orbit a half-mile away. It immediately corrected its orbital angle to be true to the equatorial orbit of the planet.

Mentar began a slow flight toward the craft, followed by Colonel Austin and then the DOE. When they got close to the vessel, they noticed that their ships were being faintly tugged toward the alien ship. Each had to reverse power to maintain their position.

"Gravity!" the colonel said. "Their ship is generating artificial gravity."

Mentar slowly positioned his shuttle in front of the Visitor, facing the windshield. He searched the bridge but could see no one. He informed Colonel Austin. The colonel began a circumnavigation of the vessel, maintaining a hundred-yard distance from it. When he reached the opposite side of the craft, suddenly, a pair of bay doors about fifty-feet tall showed a crack in the middle and then slid fully open exposing a bay about two hundred feet long and a hundred feet deep. Inside, two triangle-shaped shuttles were moored to the floor. They were about forty feet on a side. They resembled the antique delta-winged aircraft on Earth. However, there were no nozzles, jets, or propellers.

The colonel keyed his radio. "Mentar, Captain, come around to this side."

The two ships flew around the alien vessel and joined Colonel Austin in front of the open hangar bay a hundred yards away from the alien craft. The three ships came to Station-Keeping and waited, watching the open bay. Minutes later, a door at the other end of the hangar bay opened and three figures, in pressure suits, about twelve to fourteen feet tall, entered the open bay.

"Colonel!" Capitan Snyder radioed, "at the end of the bay; see them?"

"Yes. Mentar the..."

"I see them. Let's see what they are going to do."

The three aliens were bi-pedal, with arm and leg lengths the same proportion as that of a giant or a *little one*. They stepped well into the open bay and then stopped and turned to face the three-ship welcoming armada. They raised their right hands and arms in an apparent gesture of friendship.

Mentar responded immediately, slowly moving his ship toward the alien's open hangar bay. "Colonel, I'm going to move in close enough for them to see me, then motion for them to follow me downward toward the planet. If they understand, they will probably board their shuttle and comply."

"We'll follow you. Mentar, it looks like we are committed here. You may as well take them to the spaceport."

"Agreed. I'll notify everybody. You'd better radio Little One Village and any that are aboard Cosmos. Okay, approaching the open bay."

"Captain Snyder," Colonel Austin said, "you'd better notify Abbott."

"He's monitoring, sir. And just a note, Colonel, he will not fire without a direct order. These DOEs are very lethal. The US Air Force does not let anyone near them that's trigger-happy."

"Noted, Captain."

As expected, the three aliens boarded their shuttle, lifted off, exited their ship, and followed Mentar. When they cleared the bay, Colonel Austin saw the bottom side of their craft. It had three circular spots on the underside of the vessel, located near the points of its triangular-shaped hull. The spots were of an opaque-looking material. All three were brilliantly lighted.

"That's got to be the drive," Colonel Austin thought. *"Maybe some type of gravity/light pressure technology."* He saw the spaceport ahead. The aliens were dutifully following Mentar's ship. Jimmy followed a little farther behind, careful not to give the Visitors any impression that they were being crowded. Snyder's DOE was well behind him. The Captain had good judgement. If he didn't love flying so much, he'd make a good diplomat.

Colonel Austin scanned the skies above the spaceport. Captain Abbott had retreated to the edge of the tarmac and landed; engine running, no doubt. Two or three dozen people, that happened to be near the open tarmac, had grouped and were watching the ships approach. Cosmos' bridge crew were monitoring the event. They gathered to watch the landing of the alien craft.

Mentar landed his shuttle. A moment later, he opened the outer door and lowered the ramp. The alien craft lined up beside his ship and slowly descended toward the tarmac. Three twenty-four-inch beams of very bright light, being immitted from the opaque circles on the underside of the ship, appeared on the tarmac. The ship smoothly descended to touch down, then the lights went out. All eyes went to the hatch of the triangle-shaped craft. There was a brief pressure equalization sound then the ramp lowered to the tarmac and the upper door raised to full open.

A couple of minutes went by with all eyes staring at the open hatch. Mentar and Colonel Austin exited their craft and approached the visiting ship. Then, the first of the three occupants appeared in the doorway, without the pressure suit. He stood in full view of everyone as if allowing them to evaluate, and adjust, to his appearance. He himself was considering their stature as well. He showed no visual reaction to the enormous difference in Mentar's and Colonel Austin's size. Curious.

"*Gulliver...*" Mentar breathed quietly.

Jimmy looked up at Mentar,s momentary correlation of the Visitor's relative size, then to the Visitor again as his companions joined him in the doorway. They seemed to have the demeanors of seasoned travelers.

Katy watched the twelve-foot tall humanoid step into the doorway of his shuttle, then the other two join him. They were slender for their height, with a hairless head and face. They wore one-piece jumpsuits. Their skin tone was pale in color. Contrary to the Zannians, the Visitors had small ears, noses, and mouths. Their bald heads seemed to fit their general appearance very well. They were handsome of stature.

Katy glanced at Sharon. "Is everybody in the galaxy bigger than us?"

"So far," Sharon joined. "The middle one; he acts like he's been around. Confident, like his society has been involved in space travel for a long time."

"No doubt, they have. That drive appears to be a very advanced type of propulsion."

"Yes, it does," Sharon agreed. "I wonder if it has the raw muscle of our magnetic inertial system."

"Good question. One thing is evident; it does get you there, just like magnetic inertial."

Sharon and Katy glanced at Mentar and the colonel. They were approaching the alien ship.

Mentar spoke in Moon, and then repeated it in English. "Welcome to Zannia. Where is your planet?"

When the Visitors heard the Moon language, the leader motioned to one of his subordinates. He disappeared inside their ship and came back out with a silver cube about twelve-inches square. I was equipped with a shoulder strap and was hanging under his arm. The leader made an adjustment on the device and then spoke into it in an unknown language. The device reproduced the utterance in Moon.

Mentar responded in his language: "Yes, I hear and understand." Then Mentar turned to Colonel Austin: "Colonel, call one of your translators for Moon-to-English and let's move this exchange inside the spaceport."

Inside the spaceport's conference room

Mentar seated the Visitors. He instructed Kronos to access the spaceport Records Data Base and retrieve a depiction of the regional star map. While waiting for the computer to display the chart, Colonel Austin watched the aliens closely. Each time one of them looked him in the eye, he felt like a novice. He was of course, relatively new to space exploration. However, the planet he was on right now wasn't his home planet. That should count for something. He was acquainted with the business of space travel.

When Kronos completed the Data Base inquiry, Mentar pointed to the star map displayed on the conference table's large monitor. The Visitors studied it for a moment, then looked up at Mentar. The leader then pointed at a star on the chart and spoke. Upon completion of the lengthy sentence, the translation into Moon came from the underarm appliance and then from the lips of the colonel's interpreter in English:

"I am Summar; this is Aaronmar and Leeanmar. We came from this star." The voice said. The leader was pointing at Zylon/Bernard's Star. "From one of the moons of its single gas giant planet, Zylon 2. We are Zylonians."

Mentar and Jimmy leaned forward and studied the star map. "About six light-years." Colonel Austin said, "Why haven't we heard their radio transmissions?"

"That's a good question," Mentar responded. He then looked toward the Visitors and phrased the question in Moon.

The Visitors responded: "Our planet's communications have all been dark for centuries."

"Dark?"

"Hydrogen Field; non-space-polluting transmission of signals."

There was a pause while the Visitors talked among themselves. Then, the leader spoke: "In our archives, our records from millennia ago, there are accounts of when we visited both of your planets. At that time, this planet, Zannia, was almost barren with evidence of a slow recovery taking place, and the other;" the Visitor leaned forward and picked out, then pointed to, Earth, had one of its sister planets to explode and was full of debris. The record says that there were primitive occupants on one of the planets. According to the records, our explorers followed our non-interference policy."

Then," Colonel Austin said, "why did you come here to Zannia, now? What is the reason you are here?"

The Visitors spoke briefly among themselves again. "You sent the signal to us. When you activated the Sentry, we got the message."

"Mentar!" Colonel Austin interrupted, "I was right. The last control on the Module signaled the probe's maker which is obviously the Zylonians!"

After a pause, the Visitor spoke again. "When you discovered the sentry and assembled it, it's

63

programmed to display the quantum communication formula and notify us that you have it. We are commissioned by the Planetary Alliance to assist you in getting on line for Quantum Communications and into the Alliance of Planets.

"The formula," the Visitor began, "tells how you connect your communications devices to the Quantum Communications Array, not how to build the array. When you make the connection, there will be no delay in your communications at any distance, including planet-to-planet. The Array uses the hydrogen field of space, enabling all signals entered into it to be everywhere instantly."

Mentar and Jimmy looked at each other, Mentar spoke: "Quantum Communications Array?"

"It's a type of antenna that's sensitive to the hydrogen field. We have it on board our ship, ready to be assembled in a geosynchronous orbit around your planet. With your permission, we'll have our space-bots assemble it. It will download the electronic algorithms in a few hours and you'll be able to communicate through the hydrogen field in the fabric of space, instantly."

There was silence in the room for several moments as Mentar, Jimmy, and everyone else began to realize just how significant these Visitors really were. The curse of being virtually deaf in space was about to be removed. All they needed now was some tutoring on how to connect with this alien equipment, and the galaxy would magically open up.

Mentar cleared his throat. "Could we respectively ask your assistance with the Quantum Communications formula and the mechanics of connecting to the Array?"

DAN HOLT and MAX HOLT

Chapter 8

THE QUANTUM ARRAY

The armada of ships, with Mentar and dignitaries, Colonel Austin and bridge crew, DOE pilots and crews, and the representatives from the colonists, launched toward the agreed position above the planet's atmosphere. Hosted by their new friends from Bernard's Star, they all hovered in a semicircle around Zannia's best gravity-favored geosynchronous point in its equatorial orbit.

At this point, a gravity pocket, a minute difference from the surrounding gravitational influence, would keep the array stationary and in place. Some thousand feet away, twenty-four space-bots were buzzing back and forth in and out of the Visitor's mother ship. Each was scurrying into the huge vessel and coming back out with pieces of the special antenna; the Quantum Communications Array.

The space-bots looked like half-a-human, from the waist up. A head with sensors, both visual and radar, and two arms, human shaped but considerably longer. There were no legs. At the waist, there was a donut-shaped device with four of the opaque circles on it evenly spaced around it. They were glowing with light as various intensities of brightness as the machines moved about doing their jobs. They were very quick and accurate.

Katy watched one of them exit the ship's cargo bay carrying a piece of the antenna. "You know what that piece of the antenna looks like? When I was little, I used to play an ancient game called 'Ball and Jacks.' That thing looks just like one of the jacks. I used to stand them up and spin them to see if I could get all ten of them spinning at the same time."

"Those are a lot bigger," Sharon joined, pointing toward the ever-enlarging array.

"Yeah," Katy agreed, watching a space-bot approach the array with its piece of the puzzle. "that's at least thirty feet across and they're bringing out dozens of them. This antenna, or Quantum Array, must be huge."

Colonel Austin addressed the Visitors. "What about connecting the starships to the Array?"

The leader replied. "You don't need to. The starships will be connected directly to the Hydrogen Field of the Fabric of Space, just as the Array is. It's a unit, much smaller, that's mounted on the outside the hull of the ship. However, it will not rebroadcast communications. It's limited to the starship. This star system array," Summar indicated the antenna being assembled, "will transmit to personal communicators down on the planet."

"We need one of those for Earth," Colonel Austin said and paused, then looked up at Mentar, "and we need two of the starship Arrays for Cosmos and Little One."

"The fact that you are here put you on the list," Summar said. "Your solar system's Signal Modules were buried on your fourth planet, waiting for life to emerge in that star system."

"That's the one that exploded!" Jimmy said. "Mentar," Jimmy continued, "probably the reason your people didn't find them is that they didn't grow up on that planet; they came from elsewhere, here on Zannia, as a matter of fact, and you already had a Module in your possession. Solaris 4 was *a house already built*, so to speak."

DAN HOLT and MAX HOLT

Chapter 9

THE ARRANGEMENT

The Zylonnians finished the assembly of the Hydrogen Field Antenna and began the training of the locals on its use and maintenance. Soon, the calendar approached the day for Cosmos to return the research scientists to Earth. So, the planners began the process of closing the supermarket that had been supplied from Cosmos' greenhouse and hydroponics.

Fourteen of the colonists had opted to return to Earth when Cosmos departed. However, offspring, born during the journey from Earth to Zannia, and three more born during the year of research time, kept the numbers of colonists above the original 300. Jack and Brenda Owenby had settled in as colony leaders and counselors, and now considered themselves to be 'Zannians'.

The Launch of Cosmos was now a few days away. The ship was being serviced and stocked for the journey. In the air was growing excitement as the countdown continued.

Colonel Austin and the ship's company, with Mentar and his ship's bridge crew, and the new friends from Zylon 2 gathered in the main conference room. The subject of discussion was a Quantum

Communications Array for the Solar System and planet Earth. Summar readily agreed, stating that he and his crew would accompany Cosmos back to Earth and set up the Solar System as well, since they had assumed the responsibility to install and maintain Quantum Communications for the region. He also noted that they did not have another Array with them on their ship. It would have to be obtained at Communications Central, a part of Spaceport Zeta. The Arrays were manufactured on one of the small moons of Zylon 2, by androids, and stored at the spaceport.

"Spaceport?" Jimmy said, "spaceport, as in floating out in open space?"

"Yes. Spaceport Zeta is an outpost constructed at the center point of a triangle of star systems; the solar system, Alpha Centauri, and Bernard's Star. We, me and my crew, assist new planets entering the Alliance.

Both Colonel Austin and Mentar, curious about the motivation of Summar and his crew, fielded the question of why. Summar summed it up in a speech that neither Mentar and Jimmy would ever forget.

"The Planetary Alliance is a perpetual celebration of awareness. The peoples of those planets are no longer alone. Thousands of years ago, the Zylons constructed the spaceport and began the Planetary Alliance. For the first two hundred years or so, they bore the burden of its existence. But, it grew. Now androids do all the work, volunteers from the member planets staff the station. They are there because they want to be. It's a focal point for different planets

engaged in trade and knowledge-sharing. Both your worlds will enjoy a hearty welcome."

Colonel Austin was quiet for a few moments. At times, the developing situation seemed completely overwhelming. It had not been that long since Earth was a quiet little planet involved in its own affairs. Just a hundred and fifty years ago, Earthlings had learned to fly. Only two generations ago, the *bold and daring* had discovered Mentar and his kind, sheltered on Earth's moon in a survival posture. A discovery that set into motion the present saga.

Now, here they were, about to open up the galaxy and become part of a magnificent society; very big steps, very quickly. They were about to go to a spaceport that, heretofore, was only imagined in books and the movies. Once again, science fiction writers' imaginations would become real.

On departure morning, Mentar and Jimmy escorted Kaabar, Cosmos' lone giant passenger, on board and to his specially modified quarters, arranged just for him, for his ride 'home'. He would join the other giant colonists on Earth and finally get to travel to the moon to honor the memory of his grandson, who had died there when Solaris 4 exploded.

The Zylon ship waited in orbit to pair with Cosmos for the journey to the Spaceport Zeta outlined by Summar. Summar's ship would pace Cosmos at 1*G* acceleration on the designated coordinates given by Summar. Cosmos did not yet have the established grid, with its checkpoints and six-point coordinates, necessary to navigate to any destination among the local star groups. When the duo of ships reached the proximity of the Spaceport, The Quantum Cloud, Summar's ship, would escort Cosmos to docking inside the Spaceport.

Mentar, Kronos, and all the giant dignitaries, the colonists, and many that had established friendships during the tenure of Cosmos on Zannia, were at the spaceport to say their final goodbyes. In attendance were Trey Brewster and Yaccavan Kavienne, two souls cleansed by fire, that would restore their names to credibility. Their respective counselors stood ready to help them deal with their childhood demons when they came calling.

Mentar's son Menvaar Ataar was saying goodbye to his many friends that were leaving for Earth.

Jack and Brenda Owenby were well established and happy as leaders of Earth's first extraterrestrial colony. They were glad that the crew of Cosmos would get to finally get back home to their families. But they were having a small bout with homesickness and had entertained a moment of *wishing* they were going as well. They said their goodbyes to the crew and asked Jimmy to communicate to their children and grandchildren that they were missed and loved by two elderly *Zannains*.

Jimmy agreed and added, "Who knows, with this new propulsion system and the pending instant communications capability, you may be able to talk to them and convince your grandkids to come for a visit."

Brenda teared up. "I'll put that on our Bucket List."

When it came Mentar's turn, he focused on Jimmy. "I will never forget Colonel James Austin and your predecessor Colonel Marvin Andrews for the influence you've both had on my life. Return to Zannia, anytime."

"Mentar, what I have learned from you is...how to be big."

Mentar's eyes moistened. Jimmy continued. "You just may see me again. With our new equipment on Cosmos, you are just two naps and 3 months away."

Launch

The bridge crew of Cosmos sat at a conference table inside the ship, reviewing again the operating perimeters of the new Waddell Cone Protection Field and Velocity Enhancer. It mandated that if the ship was flying in formation with other ships, it must maintain at least a half-mile separation from said ships. Any closer and one or both ships could experience buffeting, due to the warping of space by the generated field of the Waddell Cone. Further, the ship should be well out of a star system before engaging the field.

Summar and crew agreed to pace Cosmos until in the proximity of Spaceport Zeta, then Cosmos would be escorted by the Quantum Cloud into the spaceport to an inside hangar, where the two starships would be moored. Then, the crew and compliment of Cosmos could enjoy shore leave and be treated to a tour of the huge city-sized habitat in space. It was their policy to welcome the new members; those who most recently found their way out of the darkness.

Summar supplied the coordinates to Cosmos' navigation crew to set course for Spaceport Zeta. They were to accelerate for one and a half light-years, then reverse power and decelerate another one and one-half light-years. They would then come to Station-Keeping, lock onto the Quantum Cloud, and follow her into Spaceport Zeta. Summar would notify the spaceport of their pending arrival and make the necessary arrangements. Cosmos' crew and ship's company would be ecstatic to see a spaceport leave the pages of science fiction and the silver screen, and become real.

Finally, Cosmos rose from Zannia's spaceport. The Quantum Cloud awaited its protégé, hovering at one mile up. Cosmos cruised to a stop, 1000 feet from the Zylon ship. Summar's mechanically-translated voice came over the intercom via the newly installed Quantum Array. "Commander, set your navigation computer on plane with Earth and Zylon with your destination at the midpoint. Fly three light-years. When you come to a stop, we'll be there to escort you into the station. Our android pilots will pace you."

Colonel Austin keyed the radio. "We'll be accelerating for one and a half light-years, then decelerating the second half."

"Understood. We'll pace you. Journey mercies, Cosmos."

Colonel Austin, caught by surprise with the snippet; "What did you say, Summar?"

"Journey mercies, my friend; it's an Earth term."

"I know," Jimmy responded. "Thank you for the sentiment.

Melvin Faulkner, telemetry, established a 'fix' on Earth's sun and Bernard's Star, and then entered into the navigation computer the place in the cosmos half-way between them.

"Navigation's set, Colonel."

Colonel Austin acknowledged. "Come in, Quantum Cloud,"

"Go ahead, Cosmos."

"We're ready to proceed on the journey."

"At your discretion, Commander. We'll see you on the other side of a sleep period."

Colonel Austin paused just briefly, then gave the order. "Launch Cosmos. In one hour, engage the Waddell Cone."

When the Waddell Generators began to hum, the ship seemed to quieten. Cosmos was now skipping by much of the labor of traversing miles of distance to destination. Space was moving aside to allow the vessel more freedom of movement.

"Colonel," navigation reported, "we see the Zylon's ship pacing us. They are giving us a wide berth. They're a little over two miles away."

Colonel Austin was quiet or a moment. "They have a completely different type of drive than we do. I'm sure it's a safety consideration, since we are employing new equipment. They stated that they would meet us there. However, Melvin, if we arrive at the agreed meeting place and there's no one there, can you get us home?"

"Yes, sir. I can plot a course to the Solar System from anywhere. When I was assigned this position, I downloaded the latest Galaxy Star Chart from the Astronomical Union and located and highlighted all the major stars in the constellations, with reference to the location of the Solar System. All I have to do is locate three of the big boys through that windshield and they will show me the way home."

"That's good enough for me. Everyone settle down and enjoy the ride." Jimmy looked at the newly added instruments on the console, reflecting the status of the Waddell Cone, then at the cluster of lights reflecting the status of the rotor pods. All were doing their jobs. He walked out into the middle of the deck and looked up at the window to the stars.

There were far distant points of light filling the transparent *eye* of Cosmos. Out of frame, on the right, was Zylon, also known as Bernard's Star, and out of frame on the left, the Sun. A spaceport lay dead ahead. He so wanted to see this wonder. The journey would take one point four years. Midpoint reverse of power must occur in eight and a half months. Jimmy was about to head for his suspended animation unit to dispense with eight months of that time, with the instructions to awaken him, if need be, for the good of the ship or it's compliment. He stopped when Mentar's voice came from the new communications system. He responded. "Mentar, hello."

"Colonel," Mentar said, "I wanted to check out our new Array. I'm on my communicator."

"Reception is good. Amazing isn't it."

"Yes. How's the Waddell Cone functioning?"

"Great. We are realizing some serious speed. Hats off to your scientists."

Aboard Cosmos

Jimmy was awakened, informed of the elapsed time, eight months, and that he was in excellent shape. He headed for the bridge for an update.

"Colonel," Katy said. "In two weeks, we reverse power. According to the instructions and cautions from the Elder scientists, we shut down the Cone generators one week from now; a week before our reversal to begin deceleration. The ship must return to its normal relationship to space. At least, that's the way they worded it."

"Understood."

Two weeks later

A mechanical voice came over the Array to the intercom: "*Please signal when you are about to cut power, so we may keep the spread between our ships to a minimum.*"

Colonel Austin keyed the radio. "Will do; where are you?"

"To your starboard, five miles."

"Acknowledge. We are prepping the ship. We'll cut power in three hours, for 15 minutes, then re-engage for deceleration."

"Standing by."

Jimmy found the Zylon ship, the Quantum Cloud, on the Near-Field Monitor. He wanted to watch it during the midpoint reverse of power.

When the mechanics of the maneuver began, he noticed that the Zylon ship did not rotate or change its posture in any way. It just suspended acceleration along with Cosmos for the duration of the maneuver, then began curtailing its velocity along with Cosmos. "Artificial gravity," Jimmy muttered. "Summar has talked about interplanetary trade. This is one thing we would be interested in acquiring. The giants, Mentar and his own, found on the moon discovered how to exempt physical items from gravity, but not how to generate it. Artificial gravity would be excellent, when hovering at Station-Keeping, in space."

Chapter 10

SPACEPORT ZETA

Cosmos, carefully prepped for weightlessness the last week of its deceleration phase, set Station-Keeping on its control panel and came to a hover. The monitors showed an object dead ahead some 200,000 miles. The Quantum Cloud, nearby, slowly took shape as it approached Cosmos, windshield to windshield. Summar became visible as his ship drifted to a stop. He raised his hand and arm in a salutation. Colonel Austin returned the gesture.

"Commander," Summar began, "according to your ship's design, you are now at zero gravity; weightlessness. We are hours away from the spaceport. Lower your landing gear and I will have our space bots attach three gravity units to them. Calculating Earth's mass, we will set them for your home planet's gravity. Spaceport Zeta has gravity close to that of Earth and many other planets in the region. When we enter, these gravity units will automatically adjust themselves to zero. You may feel slight variations during that process."

Colonel Austin was quiet for a moment. He turned to his bridge crew. "What do you think?"

"I think they know what they are doing," Bruce responded.

"Agreed," Timothy and Katy responded.

Jimmy keyed the radio. "Summar, thank you for the consideration, we're lowering the gear."

The crew watched six space bots, the same units that had assembled the Quantum Communications Array, exit the Zylon ship, in twos, each team carrying a block-shaped piece of equipment. They disappeared below the windshield, approaching the lowered tripod gears. Colonel Austin turned on the near range deceleration monitor. The robots were busy attaching the units to the middle set of landing struts.

Jimmy keyed the ship's intercom. "Prepare for gravity."

Moments later, gravity was restored.

"Cool," Sharon said.

The bridge crew all glanced at her.

The radio then came alive again with a mechanical voice. "Cosmos, follow Quantum Cloud using your proximity readouts. You will be receiving verbal updates and instructions as we approach Zeta. You do not need to respond. We are beginning our approach."

The spaceport was a tiny blimp on the monitor. The Quantum Cloud quickly gained velocity, reaching twenty thousand miles per hour. "Thank you, Mr. Frank Gordon, for these powerful rotor pods," Jimmy muttered, then ordered a half mile separation between the vessels.

The Zylon ship began slowing. Bruce matched the deceleration, flying flat and level. It was a treat to steer

Cosmos, a starship a half-mile across and thousands of tons of mass obeying a control lever, six inches long, in the hands of its pilot. He knew he would be facing some serious maneuvering soon, probably in relatively close proximity to infrastructure and maybe even other ships. The hundreds of proximity sensors mounted around Cosmos' outer hull would keep him informed of sufficient clearance. Bruce remembered his instructor pounding into him; think ahead—think ahead. The spaceport filled half the windshield, still far away.

"Colonel," navigation reported. "It's a sphere and it's over a hundred miles across. Thousands could live there."

"And just think," Jimmy responded, "we had no idea it was here. Their communications were silent to us."

"Yes, sir. I'll bet they thought we were a noisy planet."

"They patiently waited for us to grow up. Finding the giants woke us up; now it's time for some more growing."

"Cosmos, we have received clearance and instructions to enter Zeta," the, now familiar, mechanical voice said. "Close the gap to within one-thousand feet of Quantum Cloud. We will be flying through a curtain of inert gasses maintained by a gravitational field. On the other side, inside Zeta's parking bay, there's pressure similar to your home world. You may land and disembark. A small delegation will be waiting to welcome you to Zeta and when you are ready, give you a tour of the spaceport."

With the spaceport looming, the Zylon ship began to look small indeed. Dead ahead, in the sphere dominating the view, was a hangar bay opening a mile square. There were no doors on it. The opening was covered by an opaque, milky-appearing substance. It was swirling and moving as waves across a pond in a gentle breeze. It looked very similar to the surface of the drive units on the Quantum Cloud and its excursion craft. The Zylon ship had now slowed to a few feet per second. Cosmos followed.

The Quantum Cloud entered the curtain, then disappeared inside the giant sphere. Bruce, trusting his guide, allowed Cosmos to continue into the curtain. When it began passing through the special gas, the crew felt weight fluctuating until they were inside.

The Zylon ship had made a left turn and was waiting. Cosmos negotiated the turn and followed. They were flying in a vast open hallway. They could see the outer wall of the giant sphere on the left. On the right was a vertical wall, miles high, constructed in the same curving shape. The hallway went on around the vessel until the curvature gave it a visual end. The Quantum Cloud flew about two miles, passing by several open entry ways, then slowly rotated to the right, facing the vertical wall. It then approached an arched entranceway through the wall, and touched down. Bruce stopped at the next arched opening, approached, and hovered. "Colonel," he said. "The gravity units on the landing gear. What do we…"

Summar's voice came over the intercom. "Standby, Cosmos, we'll remove the gravs. Enjoy your visit. My crew and I have some work to do before departing for Earth. Please reference the various chronometers you will see throughout Zeta. Use your communicator to notify me at least eight time-units, as measured by those devices, before you are ready to launch."

"Roger, will do."

Moments later, the signal of clearance came, and Bruce landed the Earth ship in a parking spot in *wonderland*.

"Pinch me," Katy said. "I can't believe I'm really here. All my life, I've dreamed of something like this."

"I'll do better than that," Sharon responded. "I'll remind you that it's possible that, here, we may find some beings that are smaller than us."

Katy smiled, then turned and looked at Sharon. She grinned.

Colonel Austin, noting the contingency of humanoids standing just the other side of the vertical wall, the edge of the hangar bay, instructed Bruce to keep Cosmos on internal power and at the Station-Keeping setting. Bruce informed the engine room. Twenty of the rotor pods would remain online and running. Colonel Austin keyed the intercom. "Ship's Safety, what about the outside atmosphere?"

"80-20, N2-O2, just like we like it, Colonel."

"Okay, equalize pressure, open the door and extend the ramp."

The backup crew manned the bridge and Jimmy and his crew walked down the ramp. The first thing they noticed was that all the dimensions of the spaceport were large enough to accommodate giant-sized humanoids. Mentar would appreciate the hundred-foot ceilings on each level and the forty-foot entrance archways.

He turned to Sharon. "Sharon, you are a bit of a camera buff. How about being our official photographer? You can use your communicator camera to record all of this. The people back home will have a chance to see some of this. "

Sharon agreed and turned on her communicator's Camera function.

They looked up above the arched doors and noticed an etching, a phrase, in large letters, written in an unknown language. They stopped and pointed at it, noting that it was repeated over every large entrance door. An android, standing among the welcoming committee, noticed, then approached the group and spoke in perfect English. *"It's a greeting. It says:* **"Greetings and Salutations to all who enter here."**

"You speak English!" Jimmy observed.

"I speak 2071 languages." Follow me and I will introduce you to one of our station's counselors. In your language, he would be a Superintendent.

The android turned and led the group through the arched doorway. The crew found themselves in an enormous open volume of living space. The floor they were standing on appeared to fill the entire diameter of the containment sphere encompassing the spaceport. Scattered around the floor were open access doors to floors above and below, equipped with moving stairs, similar to escalators in the stores and malls of Earth.

In the distance, they could see sitting or lounging areas with humanoid looking creatures and androids in attendance. The crew was overwhelmed by the scale and magnificence of Spaceport Zeta. Jimmy was silent for a few moments. He glanced at his crew. "Let's calm down and check out what's been hidden from us for so long."

He noticed therapy-level breathing coming from some of the crew. He continued: "With all the wonders of this spaceport, we may have trouble getting some of our scientists to continue on the Earth with us."

There were two or three barely audible laughs.

There were ten more androids and a transport vehicle standing by. The vehicle would seat a dozen people. It was hovering three inches above the floor. There were several of the transport type vehicles parked along the edge of the hallway. They were all sitting directly on the floor.

An elderly male, tall and thin of frame, approached Jimmy and nodded. "I am Tholan with the Stationmaster's Corps. Welcome to Spaceport Zeta.

You may release the occupants of your ship. They are welcome."

Jimmy opened his communicator. "Bridge,"

"Go ahead, sir."

"Shore leave for everyone. Maintain the standard skeleton crew and rotate them according to ship's regulations."

"Yes, sir. Everybody is wanting to go inside and look around."

"There are androids waiting at the ramp to answer their questions and give directions."

"Yes, sir. That's one of the first things they want to see; those androids."

"As you exit the ship, the best advice I can give you is…be prepared to be amazed."

"Roger, sir."

Jimmy and crew boarded the transport. They surveyed the area. In looking up, they saw that the outer containment sphere of spaceport Zeta was transparent. The far reaches of the universe, sprinkled with stars and galaxies, were clearly visible. The brightness of the galactic core, the Milky Way, was almost blinding. The tug of the artificial gravity gave the spaceport a planet-like feel.

The transport began moving forward, then turned right at the next opening, and preceded toward the center of the 100-mile-diameter spaceport. Soon, they saw a lounging area on the left, with a sign posted by the aisle. On it was one word in an unknown language. Some of the crew pointed at it. The android pilot, noticing their body language, spoke: "*It says: Aisle Side.*" As they got closer, they could see that there was a dozen or so people sitting at various tables, some sitting alone eating something from bowls and holding a type of tablet in their other hand, reading. Others, grouped in twos and threes, were apparently talking. Katy spotted a female sitting alone near the aisle, eating from a bowl. "Colonel, could we stop for a minute? I want to talk to her."

Jimmy looked up at the android piloting the conveyance. He brought it to a stop. Katy stepped out of the vehicle and approached the table. The six-foot humanoid finished her spoon of soup, then turned and looked at Katy, holding the spoon in mid-air, frozen in interruption. Her skin was a bluish gray, with darker patches on the sides of her face. Her features were very similar to humans with the exception that her eyes were near twice the size. Her hair was short and curly. A look of question formed on her face. Katy swallowed, found her voice, and spoke: "I'm Katy Baylor...from Earth. I wanted to meet you."

The android focused on the dining lady and spoke in a different language. The lady responded in a brief statement. The android turned to Katy. "*She is a Lindian. That's a planet in the Gliese 411 System on your star charts. She's here on holiday.*"

"How could she come here on vacation when it's a year or two travel time?"

"*She came here through the wormhole system. She had a two-day transit from her planet to the Vortex, then she entered the Space Transporter and arrived here in eight days. She'll be here nine more days and then will be returning home."*

Katy was silent for a few moments, attempting to digest the unknown. What is the Space Transporter?"

"It's a magnetic field guiding system that enables ships to follow a wormhole."

Katy nodded. "Tell her I'm a computer technician and ask her what she does."

The android complied. *"She's a doctor."*

Katy nodded again and smiled, then addressed the lady. "What are you eating?"

The lady smiled, reached into a container on the table, and picked up a spoon-like tool, dipped it into her bowl, and handed it to Katy. Katy sniffed it, then slowly put it to her lips and took a sip. "It's potato soup!" She looked back to the lady's face, then extended her hand for an Earth handshake. The doctor took it, glanced at the android, then said to Katy: "I heard the announcement of your arrival. Welcome to the top vacation spot in this part of the galaxy."

Katy blinked several times and took a breath. "Thank you."

Chapter 11

THE TOUR

Earth's scientists aboard Cosmos grouped at the exit ramp to disembark and explore the spaceport. They began streaming down the ramp, heading for the arched doorway and the wonders beyond. An android stepped out into the aisle. *"Welcome to Zeta, may I help you?"*

"Do you have a restaurant?"

The android gestured toward the transport vehicles. The scientists began boarding the machines. They filled eight of them. The android liaison addressed the group. *"Your guides will be with you shortly."*

Soon, Jimmy and his bridge crew were riding the vehicle at a brisk speed. A hundred feet overhead was the next floor of the facility. Multiple viewports on both sides of the above aisle passed by the transport as they proceeded. There were banisters around them on the next floor. The ports were about a hundred feet square. One was able to see several floors up before the distance was too great for the human eye to distinguish detail.

Miles went by, then the vehicle began to slow. Ahead, there was an entranceway to a cordoned-off area. The transport passed through the doorway and stopped. There was a miles-square open area with multiple varieties of food-bearing and oxygen-generating plants, plush and colorful, growing prolifically. There were dozens of robots moving among the growth, monitoring and tending the food supply for Spaceport Zeta. The flora went as far as they could see, providing a rich freshness in the air.

"Do you ever have an insect problem," Timothy asked spontaneously.

"No," the android responded, *"they are banned. Historically, we had an incident with an insect; it was a breed of moth. A ship, that was doing research on insects in zero-G, had one escape from its test container, flying around inside their ship and was brought into Zeta. Apparently, the creature's natural instincts allowed it to find this farming area. It took twelve of those robots to catch it."*

Timothy looked up at the android. "I'll bet that was fun to watch."

"Fun?"

There was a momentary pause. "Never mind." Timothy concluded. "What did you do with it?"

"It's in the museum."

Jimmy sat straight up in his seat. "Museum?! You have a museum?"

"Yes," the android responded smoothly, *"it's on the other side of Zeta, on the top floor, 92 minutes transit time. It's nearing meal time. Shall we visit a restaurant, then proceed to the museum?"*

The crew of Cosmos looked at each other. "Yes," Jimmy said. "I want to see the menu."

"The potato soup is good." Katy offered.

The android steered the transport back to the Aisle Side lounging area. The group of scientists from Cosmos had arrived and taken up half the tables.

"Colonel!" one of them said enthusiastically, spotting the bridge crew, "Isn't this amazing! We can learn so much here!"

"Yes, yes, it is amazing," Jimmy agreed. "However, I want you guys to remember where we parked. We'll be heading for home soon."

They didn't get it. "The android pilots are showing us around. They will know how to find it."

"Okay," Jimmy said accommodatingly, as he and his crew exited the vehicle and gathered around a table. Jimmy looked up at the android. "What do we call you; what is your name?"

"I am Seven."

"Well, Seven, where do we get a menu?"

"Touch the center of the table."

Jimmy reached out and touched the table as instructed. A blue hologram rose out of it. It had some twenty entries in an unknown language. Above the listing was a red baseball sized sphere, floating. He looked up at Seven. The android reached across the table and touched the sphere. It became blue like the listings. *"State your language,"* Seven said.

Jimmy looked around at his crew, then leaned in toward the hologram. "English."

The menu blinked, then all the entries were in English. Number one was Tuber Soup.

Jimmy looked at Katy, then smiled. "You look okay; I'll take the tuber soup.

"Touch that number on the listing," Seven instructed.

The rest of the crew studied the menu. It was a mix of soups and salads of various vegetables, grains, beans and fruits. After a brief review, number one was touched five more times.

"It is delicious," Bruce said. "These androids can cook; if they do indeed cook this stuff."

"It's likely," Melvin said. "You notice that there's no meats on the menu. If they were using some type of futuristic food replicator like on the ancient Star Trek show, meat could be replicated just as easily. Space is fruits-and-vegetables country. They can be successfully grown out here, and, the by-product is O2."

"That farm we saw," Timothy joined, "was impressive. Miles and miles of plush green plants."

The scientists began boarding their transports. Jimmy watched them exit the lounge. Their faces radiated excitement. He hailed them. "You've got to see the farms; they're straight ahead."

They began the trip in an orderly caravan.

Jimmy and crew finished their meals, and then, with Seven at the helm, began their journey through the space station. Seven made a u-turn and began traversing the station again. Two miles down the main aisle, he abruptly turned right. As he cruised along, lounging-type sitting areas went by, escalators leading both up and down passed by on both the right and left sides. Soon, there appeared a large enclosed room on the right. The aisle widened in front of it, allowing parking spaces. "What is that place?" Katy inquired.

Seven brought the transport to a stop, then parked in front of the building. *"It's a place of entertainment."*

"What does that say," Timothy said, pointing at the sign above the doorway.

"The best interpretation in English is: Spirits and Song."

"Hey, Colonel," Bruce said, "let's go in there for a few minutes."

"Jimmy looked around at the crew, then smiled. "Is everybody over twenty-one?"

Seven looked at Jimmy. *"Twenty-one?"*

Jimmy smiled, paused, then looked up at Seven. "Never mind, it's an Earth thing. Let's go in the building for a few minutes."

Seven lowered the conveyance to the floor, then led the way into the establishment. When they walked through the door, the lights were lower and there was music coming from a platform on the right side of the room. The sound seemed to be a mix of Japanese and Scottish music. There were three figures on the platform with unknown instruments. They looked mysterious in the subdued light. Seven located a round table and led the party to it. They seated themselves.

"Let's order a drink." Bruce said. "We can't pass up this opportunity."

"Why not?" Jimmy agreed. "None of us are driving. However, Bruce," Jimmy added light heartedly, "I want you sober at the helm of Cosmos."

"Yes, sir," Bruce responded, grinning.

Seven was sitting at the table adding information to his vast data base; information regarding the makeup of the inhabitants of planet Earth, when Jimmy addressed him. "Seven, you place the order for us. We are not familiar with Spaceport Zeta's Spirits."

Seven immediately offered a suggestion. *"Colonel, I would recommend a barley based alcoholic drink, mixed at twenty percent spirits."*

"Sounds good to me. You buy the first round."

"Buy?"

"Sorry. Another Earth cliché. Go ahead and order for everyone."

Seven placed the order. *"You have many sayings. You are a very interesting species."*

A few minutes later an android appeared, carrying a round tray with the six drinks sitting on it. The containers were about five inches tall and two inches in diameter. They gradually widened, bottom to top. Each had a faint wisp of smoke spiraling up from the liquid. Jimmy looked at the six tiny columns of smoke. "Those are twenty percent alcohol?"

"Yes," Seven responded. *"A relatively mild drink."*

"Then, why are they smoking?"

Seven's smile was indistinguishable from human. *"That's decor. It's harmless. They drop a tiny bead into the drink that causes that effect."*

They each picked up their drinks. "We've got to propose a toast." Jimmy said, "Anybody?"

Melvin cleared his throat, looked around at the crew holding their glasses, then complied: "This may be the new era of space travel, but I want to reach back in time, to 1998, and propose a toast to the memory of the craft that got all of this started, Research One, and her crew that blazed a trail that led to this table and this moment."

They all took a cautious sip of the drinks, then looked at them and nodded approvingly.

"Well spoken, Melvin, well spoken," Jimmy said, then glanced toward the stage. The band had changed songs and playing style. The music was now slow, mellow, and relaxing, as if on cue with the arrival of the drinks. It had a waltz beat and the sound of a violin.

"I'm going to call Mentar and tell him to visit this station as soon as he can and bring Jaavienne and his guitar."

"Gallawane, in Moon" Timothy corrected, smiling, "he would be a hit here."

As the group's eyes adjusted to the reduced lighting, they began to discuss the different humanoid types seated in the club. They strangely accepted the differences in the lifeforms all around them; some quite different, others very close the to the Earth-born soul. A gradual conditioning following the dramatic discovery of some handsomely sized humanoids on Earth's moon at the end of last century.

Katy sat there, holding her drink, feeling more like a pioneer than when she first boarded Cosmos years ago. As she surveyed the room, she said. "People back on Earth have no clue about all this. The giants taught everyone that we were not the center of the universe. But this…this will stretch most of them to the edge of their understanding. How will we explain it to them?"

Timothy was shaking his head, "You can't…they'll have to see it for themselves."

As they sipped their drinks in discussion, Bruce stood to signal the waiter. He raised his hand and arm. He saw the android across the room. The waiter raised his hand in response and nodded. Then Bruce's eyes went to a table next to the wall by the android waiter. His mouth dropped open. "Oh, my God, Colonel; look!" he said pointing. Jimmy stood and followed his gesture. There were eight Earthmen sitting around a table! The rest of the group, including Seven, stood and stared across the establishment. Jimmy broke the stunned silence. "How did they get here? Come on Bruce, Seven, let's go find out."

Jimmy crossed the room with Bruce and Seven following. He approached the table. "Hello," Jimmy said, "how did you get here?"

The party of eight around the table looked confused. They remained quiet and looked up at

Seven. Seven addressed the Colonel. *"Colonel, what are you asking?"*

Colonel Austin looked at Seven for a long moment. "I'm asking how they got here from Earth; we have the only starship."

Seven studied Jimmy's countenance for a moment, then looked down at the eight seated at the table, then back to Jimmy's face. *"Colonel, these beings are not from Earth. They are from Mahan, a terraformed planet in the cluster of seven stars that you know as the Pleiades."*

Seven began speaking in the Mahans' language and explained the mistake. The Mahans looked at each other and smiled, then two of them stood and extended their hands in a closed-fist position, in a gesture of friendship. Not thinking, Jimmy awkwardly extended his in the Earth-handshake position, and then looked a little embarrassed. The two Mahans slowly opened their hands and gave an Earth handshake. Then, their whole group stood and there were Earthlike greetings all around.

Finally, Jimmy spoke. "You look exactly like us."

The Mahan looked at Seven and spoke a phrase. Seven smiled and turned to Jimmy. *"He says, no, my new friend, you look just like us."*

Jimmy's group pulled up chairs and soon both groups were talking and asking questions in their own language, creating total confusion. Seven finally clapped his android hands to get attention. When both groups stopped, he raised his hand to get the attention of another android, behind a counter. Seven shouted a request, and the other one reached under the counter and brought over a container, like a briefcase. Seven opened it, revealing 20 tiny earbuds, resembling hearing aids. As he handed them out, he looked at Jimmy and said, "These translators will enable you to speak freely with your new acquaintances."

Jimmy took one. "What are they, hearing aids?"

"No, they are inter-galactic translators. Put them in your ears and speak normally. You will automatically hear your own language, no matter what language is being spoken...any of the over 2,000 we have catalogued here." After both groups had installed their earbuds he said, "You may now talk openly. Enjoy your conversation." He pointed to a red button on the far right of the briefcase and said, "When you are ready to continue your tour, press this button and it will summon me." He then walked away.

Jimmy looked at the Mahans. After an awkward silence, he said, "I am Colonel Jimmy Austin, commander of the starship Cosmos, and this is my crew." He introduced each crew member, and then continued. "About ten years ago we journeyed from the planet Earth to the planet Zannia, to deliver an Earth colony of humans to the planet and to study its ecology for one year. We are now in route back to Earth. We encountered the Zylonian species on Zannia. They told us about Zeta and led us here. We will soon depart on the final leg of our journey home."

After a moment, the oldest-looking Mahan responded. "I am Qua; I command a Class 'C' transport from our planet, Mahan. These are the members of my crew." He introduced all eight members. Three were female.

"Well, tell us about Mahan."

After a few looks back and forth, Qua continued. "Ours is a Mahan Class-One transport ship, on a supply mission for our planet. We are somewhat amazed that your kind resembles us so closely. But, it makes sense, having read the reports from the Zeta probes, returning from your star system. As I recall, yours is the third planet from your star. It is temperate, like Mahan, and with similar rotation speed and weather systems. With almost identical atmospheres, we could live easily on each other's planets. Now that you have entered the Galactic Community, we may find opportunity to visit your home planet. You are welcome to visit Mahan anytime."

Bruce's curiosity formed as a question. "What are you doing here on Zeta? Do they have supplies for sale here, that you need on Mahan?"

Sahton, one of the females, answered. "I am the Supply Officer for this mission. There are no supplies here that we need. We must proceed farther into the galaxy to meet our requirements. We registered for entry into the wormhole when we got here, and we are just waiting our turn. Traffic is getting heavier in the tunnel as more planets join the Alliance. Of course, Zeta has to coordinate all entries to maintain required separation between all ships. Once we enter, it will take about one of your Earth-months to reach the

Dexton Star System. They have the minerals we need to continue generating our planet's atmosphere."

Jimmy and crew could hardly take it all in. Back when the giants were first discovered on the moon, the basic question, *"Are we alone in the universe?"*, had been answered. But Earth had not *really* seen the giants as *aliens;* but more like ancestors. But this...this would be different. Earth would need to be prepared for what was about to happen. Everything Earthlings thought they knew about things *out there,* was about to change.

The discussions between the two groups continued until they were laughing and sharing drinks together. Finally, Jimmy determined that it was time to continue their tour. They would not have time to see everything on Zeta before departure for Earth. After some farewell conversation, he pushed the red button to summon Seven.

Once they were all boarded back onto the transport, the tour continued.

"Up ahead are the botanical gardens," Seven reported. *"The station has added plants from just about all of the planets in this section of the galaxy."*

As they approached, the crew saw that the ceiling was open for two more floors above the garden area. It looked about a quarter mile square. Towering over the area was a Zannian tree. Its size was a definite identifying marker. It was flanked by an oak tree with a trunk about two feet in diameter. The towering Zannian tree made it look like a bush. There were all kinds of exotic growths in the garden. Climbing plants were laced through various latticework structures, in varied colors. Flowers the size of dinner plates were prolific throughout the garden. The base of each entry was enclosed with a decorative fence about a foot high. A sign was sticking up near the base of the plant. On it was the name of its home planet. There was a rich freshness and a mixture of floral fragrances in the air.

Seven slowed the conveyance and made a turn into the garden for a tour across it. About two hundred feet into it, they saw, sitting on a large bench beside the aisle, an ape-like creature about twenty feet tall. It was wearing a harness that suspended a chair just below the animal's chest. It was a completely padded chair with a foot rest and a safety cage around it. A lady, about five feet tall, was sitting in the seat provided. Hearing several inquiries, Seven brought the transport to a stop. He turned and faced the crew. *"This lady has suffered the loss of her mobility. The helper animane gives it back to her. He's the same as an assistance dog on Zylon 2 or Earth. The animanes are docile and completely loyal. They understand about a two-hundred-word vocabulary.*

"Zylon 2 has assistance dogs?" Sharon asked.

"Yes," Seven said. *"They are about twice the size of the dogs on earth, but are basically the same."*

"And the Zylonians are about twice our size," Katy added. "There's another example of that soil-content/gravity-well thing."

"It is a new field of study," Jimmy added.

"What planet has these animanes?" Melvin inquired.

"Terran. It's in the Epsilon star system, about eleven light-years away."

Seven continued the tour through the spaceport's unique garden. The scenes of the plush growth seemed to match many of the artist renditions of the huge green plants of the dinosaur era on Earth. Plush green ferns with leaves, ten-by-twenty feet, were scattered about the garden. Soon, he exited the other side, then steered the conveyance on toward the museum. The group saw the elevator up ahead. It was fifty feet square, and the shaft went all the way to the top of the dome. They looked up in awe as Seven entered the elevator platform. Their destination was near the top of the dome or sphere, known as Spaceport Zeta. The shaft, extending miles upward, with open floors on all four sides, seemed endless. Seven brought the conveyance to a stop, engaged controls that lowered the body of it to the floor in solid contact, then keyed instructions through the vehicle.

Chapter 12

THE MUSEUM

The fifty-foot square elevator gained speed until the space station levels were passing by at one-per-second. There were fifty levels per mile. At forty-eight miles, the platform began slowing. It soon came to a stop and Seven, the android chauffeur, steered the transport out of the elevator and down an aisle to an enormous doorway. The crew noticed the caption above the doorway in the, apparent, space station adopted language. "Museum?" Melvin interpreted in a guess.

"Right," Seven endorsed.

They passed through the doorway into an enormous open area. To the right were cordoned off displays. The first was an odd-looking machine about ten-by-ten feet. There were several tubes protruding from it. Seven turned and addressed the group. *"This first entry is an ancient hologram generator. The idea was for it to project three-room living quarters that could actually be used for housing. You could simply place the machine where you want to live and turn it on, then move into the facility and set up housekeeping. It worked for a short time, but then it began to affect the dwellers nervous system, causing involuntary movement and finally a debilitating condition. It had to be abandoned."*

"Interesting," Jimmy said. "A home at the flip of a switch."

Seven turned to the controls and proceeded farther into the museum. The next exhibit was an ancient satellite. The crew recognized the shape and the caption. It was Russian.

"Oh, my God," Bruce said. "That's one of the early Russian probes that flew by the Moon and went on out into space. That was about a hundred years ago. How did it get here?"

"It was spotted by a Zylonian cargo ship, drifting in space, and brought here."

Momentarily, Seven continued on along the aisle. In the next cubicle was a metal-skinned robot. It's body closely matched a humanoid, however, its face was of a plain flat design. The eyes protruded about a quarter inch. The nose was a simple button and the mouth was designed without movable lips. Seven bought the transport to a stop. *"This is one of the first sentient robots. You might say It's my great, great, grandfather; in English. He could think his way through most ordinary days. However, his processor soon became overloaded. He was a first step."*

Seven turned to his charges. *"This next area is a large open circle of exhibits of various designs of excursion craft."*

Seven proceeded into the vast circular chamber. *"This first one was donated by the Athenians. It's the smallest space-worthy shuttle in the museum."*

The crew stared at the tiny craft. Its cabin capacity was that of a crew, less than three feet tall. Sharon blurted out: "There you are, Katy!"

Katy's eyes snapped to the android. "Are there any of these people here, now?!"

"Yes, there's a covey visiting now; six of them."

"Covey?"

"Yes, they fly."

Katy stared at Seven for a long moment, then almost screamed. "There are people that can fly?!"

Seven stared at Katy while his processor reviewed an enormous data base for the best reply, then: *"Would you like to meet them?"*

"Yes!" Katy said, then leaned back with her hand on her chest, breathing laboriously; trying to digest a new piece of information that matched many deep childhood dreams.

"Let me see where they are right now." Seven touched a button on the console of the transport and spoke into it in one of his many languages. The response came in seconds. He turned to Katy. *"They are four floors down; in the library. I'll ask them to come up and meet you. They can be here in just a few minutes."* Seven activated the transport's communication system again, spoke into it for a few seconds, then released the button. *"The library will give them the message. They'll be here in a few minutes."*

Cosmos' crew disembarked the transport and stood in a group watching the entrance they had just come through into the large circular display area. Seven seemed to sense their elevated anticipation. *"They will be coming through the entrance any minute."*

They heard a high-pitched buzz, very faintly, then the Athenians appeared, all six of them. Their wings were moving so fast the crew could not see them. They looked like children suspended in midair, until the group focused on their faces. They were obviously mature, some even older, creatures. They settled down close to the floor, then the translucent, insect-like wings stopped, and they were on the floor. They folded the wings down on their backs with the tips almost touching the floor.

Seven spoke: *"Athenians, these humanoids are from Earth. They saw your craft here and wanted to meet you."* Seven then informed the crew of his explanation.

Katy spontaneously leaned forward toward the nearest Athenian and extended her hand. Instantly, the creature's wings buzzed, and it landed ten feet away from Katy.

"I'm sorry! I'm sorry!" Katy said, stepping back.

Seven rescued the moment. He spoke to the Athenian, then to Katy. *"I told him that it's an Earth gesture of hello, to hold each other's hand and shake them up and down."*

The thirty-inch tall Athenian stepped forward again and extended his small hand. Katy slowly bent forward and took his hand and shook it twice. The Athenian smiled and nodded, then spoke a short phrase. Seven interpreted: *"My name is Kaylan."*

Katy glanced at Seven, then back to the main character of her many childhood dreams. "My name is Katy. I am so glad to finally meet you. I've known you for a long time in my dreams."

The older smaller creature looked up into Katy's eyes. *"What is…dreams?"*

"Dreams are thought-adventures during sleep," Katy responded.

Kaylan reflected on the explanation for a moment. *"We don't dream. I would like to hear about your dreams."* The Athenian smiled.

The citizens of the two vastly different worlds spent half an hour shaking hands all around, keeping Seven busy with his language skills. Then, the crew watched the six Athenians take to the air and head back to their research in Spaceport Zeta's miles-square library.

"I would like to see that library too," Jimmy noted.

The crew circled the small excursion craft of the Athenians, examining it with curiosity. It was about twelve feet across and would seat four. Colonel Austin turned to Seven. "What type of power?"

"It's inertial, like the larger one they brought in," Seven said, pointing.

The crew turned and looked at the larger craft. They all recognized it at the same time. "Colonel," Bruce shouted. "That's Mentar's shuttle!"

They hurried across the floor, looking up at it. "It is!" Melvin agreed.

"What's it doing here?!" Jimmy added, turning to Seven as he approached with the transport.

Seven looked up at the shuttle, then at Jimmy. *"The Athenians, the people you just met, brought it in. That's what they are doing here. They found it adrift and could not determine who it belonged to, so they brought it here, thinking perhaps someone may recognize it. Looks like someone did. Who is Mentar?"*

Jimmy looked up at Seven. "He's a friend of mine. He's Zannian; this is his shuttle."

Jimmy spent a few minutes, explaining how Mentar's shuttle had drifted out of his starship's hangar bay during a period of weightlessness, while they were in transit from Earth to Zannia, over three years earlier. The shuttle had disappeared into deep space.

Finally, Jimmy said, "I need to get back to my ship. I want to call him and let him know his shuttle's been found."

"You can call him from any of these rest areas; there's one nearby."

Jimmy went up the ramp into Mentar's shuttle, opened the storage compartment, ruffled through the papers, located a card, then picked it up and smiled. "Mentar's soup recipe," he muttered.

Central Administration - Zannia

In one week, Mentar would celebrate his 100th birthday. His son, Menvar Ataar, was coming along nicely to assume more responsibilities of governing and, perhaps to occupy his office if, after a planet-wide vote, he managed to be the people's choice.

Mentar wondered just how big of a bash his own birthday festivities would be.

The ringing of his personal communicator interrupted his thoughts. He keyed it. "Mentar."

"Hello, big guy," came over the receiver.

"Colonel?!"

"Yes, it's me. How would you like your soup recipe back for your birthday?"

"What!"

"We found your shuttle. It's here at the spaceport, in a museum. A race of people called the Athenians found it and brought it here."

"That's amazing," Mentar said.

"Do you want to come and get it or leave it in the museum? Or, if you like, I could take it on to Earth. Then, the next time you are in town, you can pick it up," Jimmy added in an amusing tone.

"Take it on to Earth. The colonists can use it. With this new Cone system in Little One, we will be traveling to Earth ever so often to bring those that are in their last days home. As soon as Earth has the Quantum system in place, we will keep tabs on that."

"We'll take it on to Earth. Mentar, you should schedule a mission to this spaceport and bring many of your young scientists. It's absolutely amazing. Oh, one other thing. Be sure and bring Jaavienne and his instrument. There's a little club, lounge, bar, or whatever it's known as, that would enjoy his music. It's named, Spirits and Song."

"That sounds interesting. I'll remember that."

"It's good to talk to you again, my friend," Jimmy concluded.

"You, as well, Colonel. This new communication system is amazing. Good bye, for now."

Spaceport Zeta

Jimmy disconnected the communicator and then addressed the crew. "Mentar wants us to take his shuttle to Earth with us so the giant colonists there can us it. Little One is going to be routinely visiting Earth to take home their elderly who wish to spend their final days on their home planet. The Waddell Cone has opened up a new world."

The crew heard multiple chattering outside. They looked out the door of the rest area. Eight transports of scientists had entered the museum. Jimmy looked around at his crew.

"Let's have Seven make all the arrangements to load Mentar's shuttle aboard Cosmos. Then, let's see if we can get a look at the magnetic field guiding system and the wormhole vortex."

Seven contacted Tholan and apprised him of discovering the ownership of the 160-foot shuttle on display. Tholan approved of its release and notified Station Security. Seven addressed the crew. *"You have a release. Inform your pilot and I will accompany this shuttle and direct its flight out of Zeta and around to the portal where your ship is moored."*

Colonel Austin turned to Bruce and Timothy. "Can you fly it?"

"No, sir, it's not equipped with scaled-down controls.

"Understood," Jimmy said. "Looks like we will need to get it towed."

"Wait a minute, Colonel," Bruce said. "Kaabar is aboard Cosmos."

"That's right." Jimmy said enthusiastically. He opened his communicator and called the backup bridge personnel.

"Go ahead, Colonel."

Take a communicator and go to Kaabar's quarters and put him on line; I need to talk to him."

"On my way, sir."

Kaabar was having lunch; alone. The backup pilot looked up at him. "Colonel Austin wants to talk to you," he said, putting the communicator on speaker and laying it on Kaabar's lunch table.

"Hello, Colonel," the giant said.

"Kaabar, I need your help. We found Mentar's shuttle; the one we lost during our transit from Earth to Zannia. Do you have pilot's training?"

"Yes, Colonel. It's been a while since I have flown, but I flew for about twenty years transporting supplies from Solaris 4 to the moon and Mars."

"Good. I need you to fly Mentar's shuttle to Cosmos from the spaceport museum. I'll send a transport and an android guide for you. Take the elevator to the main ramp of Cosmos, then exit the ship and step through the doorway ahead and wait for the vehicle that will bring you to us."

"Roger, Colonel, will do."

A new energy flowed into Kaabar's soul. He wiped his mouth, turned, exited the cargo deck, entered the elevator, and went to the main deck ramp. He walked down it, into the spaceport, ducked and entered the facility. One of the androids standing near the entranceway, keyed his communicator. *"Attention all. One of the members of the largest known species of humanoids just entered the spaceport. He's at the entranceway of the main deck."*

Momentarily, a cargo transport approached the entranceway and stopped. Kaabar sat down on the vehicle, swung his legs around onto the deck of it and circled his knees with his massive arms. The android, as per his instructions, headed for the museum, some ten miles in and forty miles up. As the journey preceded, many creatures of all sizes and appearances waved and nodded. Kaabar, delighted, waved back accommodatingly. It became a parade, of sorts.

Colonel Austin watched Kaabar's transport come to a stop. "Kaabar, I'm glad you were onboard Cosmos. Mentar wants us to take his shuttle to Earth for the colonists there."

Kaabar entered the shuttle, then took the pilot's seat and fastened the belts. He reached under the console and flipped a switch enabling the ship's electronics, then checked the power reserve. He nodded, then opened a cover on the console and flipped four toggle switches, starting the wheel clusters built into the four corners of the ship. His pilot's demeanor, honed to perfection over twenty years of transporting many massive loads of cargo around the solar system, came back in full force. When the instruments indicated that the clusters were at full rpm, he energized the outside lights. They began oscillating around the perimeter of the vessel. The museum visitors stopped and watched the excursion craft. Kaabar checked the oxygen reserve and looked around the cabin to see that all passengers were secured for flight. "Three little ones per seat and buckle the belts."

He lifted off, then turned to the android and raised his eyebrows. Seven looked up at him and instructed. *"Climb to the roof of the spaceport, then steer to the center of the dome. There's a port there where you can exit the station; you'll need to pressurize your cabin, then fly to the other side where your starship is moored."*

Soon, Kaabar exited the spaceport, flew a quarter of the way around her and re-entered through the gas barrier, then sought out Cosmos. He held while the backup bridge crew opened the outer doors for access to the cargo bay. Kaabar expertly flew the shuttle into

Cosmos' cargo bay and set it down smoothly at one of the mooring stations.

"Thank you, Kaabar," Jimmy said. "You just paid your ticket to Earth. Come with me. Let's go call Mentar. He'll want to know that his shuttle has been, indeed, secured onboard Cosmos."

"Hello again, big guy."

"Colonel…what's up?" Mentar responded with a note of concern in his voice.

"Did you know that Kaabar was a pilot?"

"Yes. He had extensive experience, but that was a long time ago."

"He's still got it. He flew your shuttle from the spaceport museum, out through the roof and around to the hangar bays and onboard Cosmos. We have it in the cargo bay and secured. Kaabar's here with me now." He handed the communicator to the elderly giant. Mentar heard the familiar breathing.

"Kaabar?'

"Yes, Mentar. Your shuttle is in good order. It handles well."

"Kaabar, take command of it. When you get to Earth, I want you to do something for me."

"Name it."

"Pick a crew for the shuttle from the colonists. Petition the little ones for a guppy to accompany you when you go to the moon to visit the Memorial, then get that Moai, the sentinel that was at the entrance of the dome, and move it to Mentar City."

Kaabar turned and looked at the colonel. "You've got the guppy," Jimmy responded, "plus we'll join your armada with one of our shuttles as well."

Kaabar keyed the mike. "It's all arranged, Mentar."

"Thanks, Kaabar, say hello to everybody for me."

DAN HOLT and MAX HOLT

Chapter 13

THE LIBRARY

The compliment of Cosmos settled down for an overnight stay at Spaceport Zeta. All had visited in the floating city. A complete tour of the space station would take months. It was a hundred-mile diameter sphere of honeycombed areas. It had taken centuries to construct thus far and its development was ongoing.

Summar, commanding the Quantum Cloud, had notified Colonel Austin that all arrangements had been made and the needed equipment was on board his ship for transport to Earth. Jimmy had not sent Earth a message. Had he done so, Cosmos and the Quantum Cloud would arrive well ahead of it; hence, pointless. In less than two years, Earth would be making a giant leap into the future. Alexander Graham Bell would have been very impressed.

The next morning, Colonel Austin and his bridge crew exited Cosmos and entered the transportation hallway. The androids were waiting. Jimmy looked around and did not see Seven. He approached another of the attendants. "I don't see Seven, our guide from yesterday."

"He's on his way. The Athenians summoned him earlier. He's finished there and now on his way here. He will arrive in about eleven minutes."

Momentarily, Seven arrived with an empty transport, then slowed and stopped beside the bridge crew. They boarded and seated themselves. Seven got up from the driver's seat and approached Katy Baylor. *"I have a message for you from the Athenian you met yesterday."* He handed her a four by six-inch flat screen device about a quarter inch thick. There were three buttons displayed on the lighted screen. *"The middle one will receive it in English,"* Seven added. *"For your response, the left button is NO and the right is YES."*

Katy looked at the colonel and around at her crewmates, then reached up and touched the center button. The screen changed.

Will you have lunch with me at Aisle Side, 11:00 o'clock?
Kaylan

Katy took a couple of labored breaths, touched her chest with her left hand, then looked up at Seven.

"Touch a button for your answer."

Katy paused. "Colonel, what do you think?"

"Young lady," Jimmy said, struggling to keep a straight face, "I'm not your father."

Her crewmates all laughed, looking at her. Katy looked up at Seven again, then reached up and touched the button for YES, then extended the device toward Seven to return it.

"You will need that. When he speaks, it will be on your device in your language. He has the same to interpret your utterances."

"Thank you, Seven."

Seven seated himself, activated the transport and turned it around, then quizzed the crew for their interests for the day. Colonel Austin outlined their request. "First, let's visit the library and see how It's laid out, then we would like to know more about the Magnetic Field Guidance System and the wormholes and their connection with the Vortexes at each end.

"Understood," Seven responded. *"First, we'll tour the library; it's quite extensive, then, following lunch, we'll transfer to an excursion craft and I'll take you to view the Vortex. It's five miles from the spaceport in the direction of Zylon, or Bernard's Star. At that point, I will describe the field guidance system."*

Seven turned and began the journey across the spaceport. Soon, the Aisle Side restaurant passed by on the left. Katy searched all the tables. Sharon noticed. "Katy, it's not even 8:00 o'clock yet. Relax, you are getting a gift of a lifetime. You are going to get to visit with a member of a completely different civilization. A vastly different lifeform."

"I don't know why I am so nervous."

"To be sought out by a member of a different world is reason to be nervous. I envy you. Ask him about their women," Sharon concluded.

"I have a million questions, that being one of them," Katy responded, settling down.

Seven continued to the middle of the spaceport, and then turned right for two miles. Soon he approached an elevator, steered the transport into it, lowered the transport vehicle to the floor, and entered some commands into the console. The elevator sped upward for several miles, then slowed and came to a stop. Seven exited, turned left, then entered the vast library.

The crew looked across its expanse. It was over a mile square. There were hundreds of aisles of digital equipment, view screens, and even hard bound books. The knowledge of the galaxy was concentrated in this assemblage. There were dozens of beings occupying the cubicles and cordoned-off compartments.

"What a treasure trove!" Sharon exclaimed. "Everything one would want or need to know, is here."

"Encyclopedia Galactica," Melvin mused. "Soon, we will be listed here. What will be the writeup on us and Earth?"

The crew contemplated the library, it vastness, and the various beings there, seeking information. Somehow, they knew that the day would come when they would be back here, searching the millions of tidbits of information, for something significant; something important.

Seven cruised slowly down the main aisle from the entrance door for several hundred feet, then brought the transport to a stop. He gestured to the right. *This area is dedicated to information on the Wormhole*

Travel System. All the technical information is here and the maps of the vortexes, or junctions, around the galaxy. The vortexes are the stations where you can enter and exit the system. Would you like to see the map?

"Yes," Jimmy responded.

Seven ordered their transport to settle to the floor, then entered the section and indicated a ten-foot by ten-foot monitor. He activated the equipment and the screen lit and began processing an image. In a few moments, there was a multicolored map, littered with stars and planets. The stars were represented as black circles, each with an eight-digit number beside it; the planets by hollow circles, each with a six-digit number beside it. Melvin noticed that a few of the planets displayed had only four numbers beside them. "Why are some of the planets represented by only four numbers?"

Seven looked at the screen again. *"They are not in the system yet. They don't have Quantum Communications. They are still in the dark."*

There were blue hologram tunnels meandering through space among the displayed planets and stars with an occasional interruption of a red square. The crewmembers were mesmerized by the giant display.

"Where's Earth?" Bruce said.

Seven stepped over to a piece of equipment sitting at the base of the monitor and typed in a code. An average-size planet, with only four numbers, in the upper left quadrant of the display, began blinking. It continued for one minute, then went back to a solid display. There was a red square near it. Bruce took a breath. "We're close to a vortex!?

Seven nodded. *"Yes. It's just inside your Oort Cloud, not too far from the outermost edge or your Kuiper Belt."*

"Oh my God!" Melvin said. "That means that other beings in starships have been flying through the edge our Solar System!"

"Yes, for thousands of years."

"I've got to see the vortex here at the spaceport." Jimmy said. "Is the vortex in the solar system visible?"

"You would have to be fairly close to it, but, yes. When we visit the vortex here after lunch, I'll go into the world of wormholes more thoroughly."

With that, Seven boarded the transport again and continued down the main aisle of the library. *"Up ahead is where the individual planet information is located. There's a specific enclosure for each planet which contains all the known details of that planet. There's now fifty-four specific study areas. If you wanted to know more details for, say, Zylon, or Athene, you pick that enclosure and it's all there."*

Seven drove on for a few moments in silence, then slowed and stopped in front of a two-story enclosure more than a thousand feet square. *"This might interest your scientists. This area contains all known forms of propulsion from ancient rockets to gravity assist light pressure."*

"Do the records include Magnetic Inertial Propulsion?" Jimmy asked with just a touch of pride.

"Not yet. It's coming," Seven responded, with just a hint of a smile.

With the informative sampling of the spaceport library, the crew then headed for Aisle Side to drop off Katy for her meeting with Kaylan, and then on to a Seven-recommended vegetable deli two floors above the Aisle Side lounge.

Aisle Side Restaurant

Kaylan, the Athenian, was waiting at a table, well away from the aisle. Katy spotted him and stepped out of the transport. It pulled away and continued down the aisle. Kaylan was sitting on a special chair that was raised to accommodate his statue. Katy made her way over to the small table and nodded to Kaylan, then seated herself. She laid the tablet translator in front of her and then spoke. "Thank you for inviting me to lunch. I did so want to learn more about you and your species; and you personally."

Kaylan glanced at his translator and then to Katy and smiled. "I must hear about your dreams; the fact that you mind works while you are sleeping fascinates me."

"We call it dreaming. The mind does a lengthy adventure, say an hour, in a matter of seconds, and it seems absolutely real. The brain releases a chemical that paralyzes the body, so we don't act out the adventure going on in the mind."

"Fascinating. Tell me about one of those adventures and, when did you see me in your dream?"

"In one of my dreams, I had wings, like you. I was flying through the woods—the forest, and you were chasing me. Katy paused, momentarily experiencing emotion.

Kaylan looked up from his tablet. "Did I catch you?"

Katy read the tablet and blinked, and then a blushing sensation briefly swept her face. She was quiet for a moment. Kaylan raised his eyebrows.

Katy smiled. "I don't know. I woke up."

"You cannot control these dreams?"

"No. Some of our scientists say that it's a built-in function of the mind, to clear its memory banks of piecemeal information by forming it into a story."

Kaylan was quiet for a moment, then looked at Katy. "Well, Katy Baylor, I would have tried."

"Tried what?"

"To catch you."

The android waiter appeared at the table with two beakers of a clear juice with just a hint of greenish color. He sat one in front of each of them. Kaylan spoke: "I ordered us a mixed fruit wine. I hope you like it."

Katy picked up the beaker, sniffed the wine, then took a sip. "It's delightful."

"Shall we order?" Kaylan said.

"You order," Katy said. "I'll have whatever you are having.

"On a fruit dish, what is your preference; sweet or tart?"

"Either."

"You are easy to like, Katy Baylor."

Kaylan placed their orders for a fruit dish—tart. Momentarily they were quiet for a sip or two of wine, then Katy looked up at Kaylan. "I'm curious. Since you fly, do you live in the air, like the birds?"

"No. Our houses, our dwellings, are on the ground. There are a few of our young that live in the air for a time. But, as time goes by, they move to the ground. There's a few exceptions, of course."

"Tell me about your women, your females. What are they like? I have a friend that told me to ask."

"Well, our females are slightly larger than us males. We hatch from eggs which is rather unique, as you know. Eons ago, the females tended the eggs; kept them warm; until they hatched. That's probably why they are larger than the males, originally, to protect the eggs. Now, when the females lay the eggs, they take them to a central incubator where they are kept until they hatch. The parents are notified on hatch day and go to the hatchery hospital for the event and take them home."

"That's amazing. What is the average lifespan on your planet?"

"About 300 years; and yours?"

"About a hundred years; I'm 35 now."

"A youngster; I'm 206. On my planet, you would be about a hundred. Considering the equivalent longevity.

DAN HOLT and MAX HOLT

"I would love to visit your planet one day."
"You have a standing invitation."

Chapter 14

THE VORTEX

Seven turned right for a mile, then turned left and stopped at a bay with three shuttle-type craft sitting a few feet apart. He invited the crew to enter the first one. He took the pilot's seat and manipulated some controls. A faint hum found their ears.

"That's a familiar sound," Bruce commented.

The craft lifted off, then proceeded to the ceiling of the sphere and then to the center of the dome. Moments later they were in space. Seven turned toward a bright star and began forward flight. He indicated the brighter point of light in the expansive night. *"Bernard's Star,"* he said.

Jimmy's eyes went to the rearview monitor as the magnificent sphere, created by an advanced civilization, receded behind the spacecraft. It was a harbor in the night, a glowing orb, a place for the children of the universe to pillow their heads and rest. For a moment, he was overwhelmed with emotion. There was so much to know. He focused his attention ahead again, looking for…he could not imagine what it might be. It had been referred to as a Vortex. He glanced at the rest of the crew. Jimmy noticed that they occasionally checked the rear-view monitor as a reference. How far have we come? How big is it? What will it look like?

All eyes of the crew were searching ahead in anticipation. Then, completely by surprise, the vortex appeared ahead. It was cone-shaped and about a mile across. It resembled white clouds that seemed to be pulsing and tumbling in on itself. Looking straight into the center hole itself, it seemed to have no end, like it went on as a tunnel forever. Seven brought the ship to a hover, then turned to the crew. He would remember the look of amazement on their faces.

Chapter 15

DEPARTURE

Colonel Austin contacted Tholan, the Stationmaster who had made them feel at home, and thanked him for a hardy welcome and the accommodating guides that made Cosmos' visit so informative and rewarding. As Earth's first ambassador, he expressed appreciation for the Quantum equipment that would finally put the Solar System online with the rest of the galaxy, bringing it out of the dark. He petitioned all to be patient with the indigenous peoples of Earth, allowing them time to adjust to a new open world. Earth had learned to live in the dark, therefore, for a while the light would be blinding. He assured them that Earthlings were a curious and energetic species that, in time, would make considerable contributions to the galactic community. Colonel Austin, commanding Cosmos, bade Spaceport Zeta farewell.

Cosmos and the Quantum Cloud began moving slowly away from Spaceport Zeta. Jimmy keyed his ship-to-ship Comm. "Summar, follow me and I'll show you my world."

The ship began accelerating. At five million miles, the Waddell Cone was engaged, and Cosmos was on her way home. Jimmy had three things on his agenda:

to complete a review of Cosmos and its status, make a call to Mentar for a mutual update, and take an eight-month nap.

The bridge crew settled in at their familiar stations that, somehow, seemed new. The experiences at Spaceport Zeta had left them enlarged and enlightened and challenged. There was much in their futures. Things wonderful. Things worthy of study and application.

The intercom came alive: "Katy Baylor, you have a package in Communications; repeat, Katy Baylor, you have a package in Communications."

Katy looked around at her colleagues, then got up and headed for that department. When she stepped through the door, one of the staff turned from his monitor and pointed to a package about a foot square wrapped in a silvery colored paper-like wrapping. "One of the androids gave it to security just before we launched. He said it was for you."

"Who is it from?"

"We don't know. There's no name on it."

Katy, her mind beginning to stir with logic, headed back to the bridge to open it. She removed the wrapping and opened the container. Inside, wrapped in a snow-white cloth was a crystalline statuette of a winged Athenian, about twelve inches tall. There was a tablet in the box with it. She picked it up. The screen came on with a small button highlighted in the middle of the it. She touched it, and read:

Katy Baylor, dream for me and I shall fly for you. Farewell, my friend from Earth.

Kaylan

Katy looked at the statuette with moist eyes. "It's beautiful. The wings are attached where our shoulder blades are located on our backs." The bridge crew looked at the sparkling crystalline figure in awe. Sharon reached out and touched it. Katy handed it to her. Sharon looked it over, rubbing her hand the length of the wings. She passed it on. Each of the bridge members admired the piece. It made its way back to Sharon.

She looked it over again. "What a treasure. Katy, the world needs to know about this; they need to see it. It will help them understand when you tell them about Kaylan and his world."

"I know," Katy said. "Although it's tempting, I cannot keep this to myself. It has to go in the Space Flight Center Museum for all to see."

"The museum staff will interview you for all the information they can get to display with it. And, Katy, you have to tell me all about your lunch with him. What he said; everything."

Almost Home

The pale blue dot finally appeared on Cosmos' long range monitor. It was *HOME*...a place the crew had not seen in twelve years. They had known that before leaving Earth on their mission, another ship was on the drawing board. It would be a great addition to the Gordon Space Flight Center. It would take almost a decade to complete.

As expected, during the research year on Zannia, they received a one-way information message that the new starship, a sister ship to Cosmos, was about half finished. A logical step for a space-traveling species.

Now Cosmos, almost home, was carrying all the blueprints and instructions for the Waddell Cone. It would be incorporated into the new starship's design.

When they arrived on Earth, no doubt, there would be a different president, probably a different NASA administrator, many more saucer type vehicles, and significantly fewer cars. It would be a society fast adapting to the space age. And now, Cosmos and the many minds aboard her, would accelerate that transition.

Just before entering the Solar System, Jimmy alerted the crew and Summar on the Quantum Cloud, that he was going to disengage the Waddle Cone. As the fabric of space unwrapped from around Cosmos, she dropped well below light speed.

In just over three months, they would arrive. Many messages were now being beamed ahead, during the final months of deceleration, to the current administration and to NASA, informing them of the impending arrival of the Quantum Cloud and the purpose of her visit. History would record this as the century of giant leaps forward for the peoples of planet Earth. The world would be informed of the vast improvements that came home with Cosmos. Things seen, and things learned at Zeta would astound all on Earth. Some would be disturbed and even upset…until they finally embraced the reality that humans were *NOT* the center of the universe. The little pale blue dot, that humans called home, was gravity-locked to just one of over 250 billion stars in the Milky Way Galaxy. It was just skirting the outer edge of the Orion Arm of but one of over 100 billion galaxies in the universe. It helps to have *perspective*!

Soon, friends from Bernard's Star would be installing communications equipment that would finally open up the Milky Way Galaxy to Earthlings. And the folks on that *pale blue dot* would watch it happen on TV. The Giants' Channel would finally be at the top of the ratings, again. Another group of giants, not so big this time, would meet the *little ones*; not so little this time. The public's response would be…interesting.

The crew was looking forward to arrival, when everyone aboard would have some time to settle back in to Earth, and their families and homes. Shore leave would be short for some, since there was already another mission to the moon scheduled. It would create some more delightful programming to be aired on the NASA/GIANTS' Channel. The channel already held a sizable viewership, as it had ongoing monitoring of the Mars restoration. But now, it would have new and fresh programming for its faithful.

DAN HOLT and MAX HOLT

Chapter 16

ARRIVAL

Colonel Austin activated the Quantum Communications equipment and entered the code for Zannia. Kronos answered. "Greetings, Colonel."

"Kronos, may I speak to Mentar?"

"He's in the hospital, Colonel. Hold on and I'll patch you through."

Mentar answered. "Hello, Colonel, you should be just about home by now."

"Yes, we are about three months away. What are you doing in the hospital?"

"I experienced some dizzy spells. The doctors said I was putting in too many hours. We've got a new starship under construction and we are expanding the spaceport here."

"You must learn to delegate, my friend, delegate. You are over 100 years old."

"That's what the doctors ordered. And, I'm going to do that. You and your crew must have made a good impression at the Zeta Spaceport. Apparently, Kaabar was a hit. We got an invitation through our Quantum equipment to visit the station, and they would like some information on Zannians for their library records. When I get out of here, I'm going to set up a visit there."

"I recommend it. Take in the farms, the museum, and don't forget the Wormhole Vortex near the station."

The Earth was growing rapidly on the monitors. It had a special beauty to its returning children and a new page of experience to the visiting Zylons, descending minutes behind Cosmos. Soon, the Space Flight Center and Mentar City combined metropolis, now matching the size of nearby Wichita, took shape with its thousands of onlookers circling the landing zone. Scattered about were a number of saucers.

Sitting next to the enormous maintenance shop was the old cargo transport ship, the Mary Lou, undergoing routine maintenance. Its sister ship, the Maxie Gene, and the spaceship Discovery, having taken a thirty-day hiatus from Mars duty, were sitting on the tarmac awaiting the return of Cosmos. They had been housing and supporting a large construction crew that was involved in erecting an enormous dome over Cydonia on Mars. It would be decades before their ecological efforts would bring Mars' atmospheric pressure up to livable, so the dome was necessary in the interim. But, one day....

The entire planet was abuzz with the pending arrival of Cosmos' seasoned space farers. Everyone wanted a chance to see first-hand a new race of *semi-giants.* Country delegations and media outlets from around the globe were jockeying for space around the Space Center. The Quantum Cloud would be the first *real alien ship* Earthlings had ever seen. The fact that the Zylons appeared to be distant cousins of the si-fi aliens of old had fostered both curiosity and fears.

Shortly after Cosmos came to rest, the Quantum Cloud, about half her size, touched down beside her on the tarmac of the Frank Gordon Space Flight Center. Cosmos had brought home a friend.

When the starship opened the ramp and the bridge crew walked down it, cheers went up in a cacophony of sound. Then, the focus went to the ramp of the Quantum Cloud. A hush fell on the crowd as they anticipated their first look at a new set of giants.

Summar and his colleagues stepped out on the ramp, paused, and then raised their arms and waved at the crowd. They were greeted with applause and mixed verbal greetings. Up beside the welcoming committee from Mentar City, they looked small. Summar, in his experiences of meeting new civilizations, had learned to *work the crowd.* He deliberately looked up at the colonists, came to attention and saluted. The crowd cheered.

Colonel Austin approached the president, the NASA chief, and the two leaders of the giants' colony, making use of the custom-built platform one more time. President Benjamin Montgomery addressed Colonel Austin and his bridge crew.

"Welcome home, Colonel. Your transmissions over the past decade have been full of adventure and discovery. Digesting it all will take another decade. Great job."

"Mr. President, a whole new world is about to open up for planet Earth."

"I know. I have discussed this development with our scientists. They are eager to get introduced to this mode of communication; especially those that are dedicated to the study of Quantum Entanglement."

"This is Summar," Jimmy said, glancing up at him. "He and his colleagues will counsel them on the equipment and its operation and maintenance. They have space bots, interesting machines, that will assemble and activate the Quantum Communications Array in orbit around Earth."

The president stepped to the edge of the raised platform and extended his hand to Summar. The giant shook his hand, then reached down and activated the silvery cube hanging under his arm, and addressed the president in his native tongue. A second later, the cube translated the ongoing conversation.

"I'm glad to meet you, Mr. President. Your starship, and its personnel, are impressive. Welcome to the Quantum world. We look forward to interacting with your planet."

"Thank you. We feel privileged to be granted this consideration. We are a young and curious species and wish to learn and grow."

Summar nodded and smiled. Jimmy looked at the president, impressed by his diplomacy, and agreed with the sentiment.

Those who had arranged a tarmac party, back when Little One had arrived years earlier to pick up the

Elders that had been dredged from the sea, stood by in the wings, waiting for a nod, as if it was only yesterday. They knew this party would require the entire voluminous maintenance hangar at the Space Center. The Moonies, the band that had played years earlier with Jaavienne and his giant band, upon being informed that the two starships were closing on Earth, arranged and began practicing a medley for the occasion.

The party, celebrating the arrival of Earth's star voyagers, was quickly being arranged and the *Welcome Home* party became the event of the decade. The space travelers and their alien partners were lavished with praise and food during the festivities. All Space Agency personnel, the colony of giants, family members of the travelers and a mix of world dignitaries partied well into the night. In many ways, for planet Earth, it was a *coming out of the darkness* party.

Sharon, the crew's resident photographer, had compiled her photos and videos of Zeta and showed them on a large screen projector. The media rebroadcasted the presentation around the world. **Amazement** was too benign a word to describe the crowd's reaction. NASA would soon be deluged with a volume of Astronaut Applications that would take months to sort through. The young had been inspired to *reach for the stars*.

DAN HOLT and MAX HOLT

Chapter 17

THE COMMUNICATIONS ARRAY

Summar and colleagues, traveling in a hastily equipped guppy shuttle, escorted by two shuttlecrafts, were being flown country to country to meet heads of state and their peoples. The Zylonians were overwhelmed by the diversity of peoples on Earth. A planet unique from the many in the Milky Way Galaxy. Different people, different colors, different cultures, different life-ways, and different reactions to the *new* giants.

The population of Earth was becoming known as an extension of the giants of Zannia. All wondered where the *little ones* would be in a thousand years; if they would ever claim their rights as sentients, and be recognized as citizens of the universe in their own right.

Summar was certain that the citizens of the Solar System would climb to their own plateau of recognition, and beyond. He was glad to be part of one of the steps toward that realization.

Earth orbit

A full circle of ships, dozens of them, were watching the show as Summar's space bots again assembled another Quantum Communications Array. All the major countries were in attendance. Jimmy wished that the original crew of the infamous Research One was here to see Earth become part of a galactic alliance. They had boldly taken the first steps to climb out of isolation and into the light. Now, they had all passed away. Their images and their ashes were preserved in a memorial at the Frank Gordon Space Flight Center.

To further honor their memory, as the ones who had actually taken the first step toward the stars, Jimmy requested permission, and the families approved, of transporting a small container, with just a few of each one's ashes, deeper into the galaxy and releasing it in open space. Jimmy and his crew would take the container on their return trip to Zeta. Then, during their Quest, deeper into the galaxy, they would hold an appropriate ceremony and release the container into space. The pioneering heroes would then become permanent members of the galaxy they had only dreamed about. They would orbit forever among the stars.

When the Zylonians finished their work, they returned to the surface and took the final step, assigning a band of Quantum Communications frequencies to Earth. Communicators on the planet, that would be used to access the new system for interplanetary communications, would have to be modified with the codes necessary to be part of the system. It didn't take the Zylonian engineers long to install the modifications on all communicators available to them locally; government and Space Agency officials and the leaders of the giants in Mentar City. They then left additional small electronic modules and the instructions to build more and eventually modify all communicators on Earth.

Finally, after an appropriate ceremony, Summar led Jimmy to a large green button on the panel that had been installed at NASA to monitor the status of the orbiting Array. Jimmy was given the privilege of pressing the button that would connect Earth to everything... *out there*. To thunderous applause, the Quantum Communication Array went online. Before the sun went down, the communicators on Zannia began ringing.

Some of the first to call were Jack and Brenda Owenby's children and grandchildren. There were many tears and laughs as they were updated on the Earth-side growth of the Owenby family. The companion data circuit allowed real-time sharing of photos from both ends. Jack and Brenda shed a few tears at the photos of their first great grandchildren. The family couldn't get enough of the images of the giant's planet and Little One City.

Grandkids Jackson and Hannah were the first young ones in line to share how they were now *all grown up*. When granddaughter Lilah got on the line they celebrated her recent graduation with a Master's Degree in Education Administration. Lilah said how proud she was of Grandma and Grandpa and would love to join them in the colony someday. Brenda instructed her to go to the NASA Administrator and remind him that the Zannian Colony had been promised priority for anything they needed. She said their biggest need now was a Headmaster for their growing Colony School.

Lilah made the request of NASA and Colonel Austin soon received orders to make room on his next mission for Zannia's first official Head Master and school teacher.

With their task completed, Summar prepped the Quantum Cloud for launch at the Frank Gordon Space Flight Center. The Zylonians, before saying goodbye and heading home, went about the business of providing to maintenance personnel the information on the Array and the instructions for keeping the Array serviceable. When the meeting finished in the Maintenance Office, Jimmy called Summar aside and got his personal communicator code and the personal codes for Tholan and Seven, at Zeta. There was a desire creeping into his soul to aggressively follow his new commissioning…to search out the original source of the Moai; where they had come from and why they mirrored the likeness of the Zannians. There was, without a doubt, an identifying match.

Finally, Colonel Austin, his bridge crew, the President, the NASA Administrator, and a delegation from the Zannian colonists in Mentar City, bade farewell to Summar and colleagues in a ceremonial goodbye, with a hardy *thank you* for lifting the curtain on the galaxy for planet Earth. Summar and company rose into the heavens, set course for Bernard's Star and headed home.

As Jimmy watched them go, he committed himself to work with the Space Agency to ready all of Earth's spaceship crews for transiting the wormhole system throughout the galaxy. That step would be as significant as when the first cognitive man discovered fire.

DAN HOLT and MAX HOLT

Chapter 18

KAABAR

Kaabar's selected crew was excited about a mission to the moon and the opportunity to see the Memorial once again. Plus, they were going to retrieve the Moai, the original one that was placed on the Moon, back when it was regulating the tides of Zannia, then, had been installed as a welcome at the entrance to the lunar arcology on the moon over 50,000 years ago. They would transport it to Mentar City and erect it as a sentinel, signifying who they were.

Colonel Austin and his crew, flying Shuttlecraft One, stood by on the tarmac with Guppy One and her crew, waiting for Kaabar to signify launch. Kaabar was relishing the moment. He was no longer old; he was back! It breathed new life into his being. However, he knew that his exploits, whatever they may be, would need to be soon.

He gave the order for launch. The three ships left the tarmac and, in a smooth ballet, positioned themselves in a triangle formation, a hundred feet apart, each facing the triangle's center.

Jobbers had long since cleaned up the skies of Earth. The effort had been extensive and beneficial. Rarely, now, were there stories of a ship being nicked by a rivet or fleck of paint that had escaped the process and was still in orbit. But, all in all, the blunderbuss rocket days were gone, and the remnants of their use were virtually eliminated.

The three ships accelerated at .46G, as per the capabilities of the Zannian shuttle. As they traversed the highway to Luna, a conference took place. A conference for planning to broadcast both these historic events to Earth and the viewership of the giant's channel that had been established when the giants were first transported to earth, decades ago. Colonel Austin's crew had a new transponder onboard, to install at the tunnel entrance on the moon. Then, the ships would be positioned to beam the signal from the Memorial marker to the signal booster for relay back to Earth.

The viewers on earth would get to witness the special ceremony and then, the recovery of the coveted Moai. The lunar Moai was the original one from Zannia. It differed from the Easter Island statues carved from volcanic stone, in that it was made of a more solid and smoother material. It was before Easter Island. It was before modern man. It was in the likeness of the Zannian citizens. It was a deepening mystery and, being stone, it offered only silence.

The Moon

Kaabar and his associates stood around the Memorial dedication marker, the marble monolith on the moon, engraved with the names of the entombed.

He rubbed his hand across his grandson's name. He read the engraving, in Moon, on top of the memorial. Then they stood quietly for a few moments. Jimmy and his crew stood lined across the windshield in reverence.

At length, Kaabar, finding his voice, ordered the crew back aboard his shuttle and preceded back out the tunnel and up out of the entrance crater. He steered the craft to the area where the huge entrance to the dome was known to have stood. Kaabar, in his active days had flown through it many times with payloads for the Arcology. He recognized the foundation of the entranceway.

As they got closer, they spotted the Moai, half covered with dust, lying on its side. The guppy pilot saw the prize and landed his ship in line with the heavy carving so that four of the giants could lift it and walk it straight into the cargo hold of the guppy.

Kaabar's men, still suited, donned their helmets and exited the shuttle and approached the Moai. Two of the team wiped the dust from the statue, then turned it on its back. With two on each end, they picked it up and worked it into the guppy's cargo hold and secured it. The pilot closed the ramp. When Kaabar's crewmembers re-entered the shuttle, he addressed Colonel Austin.

"Colonel, we are about a quarter-mile from the Extension Research Lab. It was located to the right of the entranceway, close to the wall of the dome. I delivered to it many times. There were two students working in that lab. They were training under the six scientists assigned to it. Were those students rescued and, maybe, the scientists recovered from there when the little ones rescued the 1200 students?"

"I don't think so," Jimmy said. I've heard nothing of an extension lab. What were they working on?"

"Extending the range of the sleeping gas that we used for suspended animation. They were trying to concentrate it, so we could carry less volume of gas to reach any destination. The idea was to require less space on the ships for the suspended animation agent. They wanted it to be more potent; hence, less would be needed. The lab was built underground, like the main lab we just left."

"Show me where it was."

"Follow me." Kaabar began cruising along the perimeter of the wall, the traces of which were left on the ground. At about a quarter-mile, he stopped his shuttle. "It was here, right here. I remember that column," he said, indicating a damaged post sticking out of the surface.

Colonel Austin pulled up beside Kaabar and examined the area ahead. It was scattered with debris, broken panes of glass from the nearby shattered dome, partial support beams and other trash and debris, all of which was covered in lunar dust.

Kaabar got up from his seat. "I'll suit up and go out there. I think I can find it."

"Kaabar, wait," Whanlaar, the ship's navigator said. "Let me go. If something goes wrong, I'll have youth on my side. You can monitor and direct me through the windshield."

Kaabar hesitated for a moment. "Okay, you and Maalan," Kaabar said, indicating his co-pilot. "And, I want you both tethered."

"Yes, sir."

Jimmy, monitoring the intercom, turned to his crew. "Timothy, you and Sharon, suit up; affix tethers, and standby."

Maalan and Whanlaar, exited the giants' shuttle and approached the debris-filled area. Maalan picked up a piece of a beam and tossed it to the side. Whanlaar joined in. They busily began clearing the slightly sunken area. Soon they had a pile of debris to the right of the depression. The last of the obstructing material was a square beam of black material, ten inches square and about twenty feet long. One got on each end. They lifted it from the surface. Suddenly, the surface collapsed under the navigator, Whanlaar. He dropped out of sight. The beam dropped back to the surface. His tether snaked through the sand, then stopped, still slack. Maalan dropped his end of the beam and hurried over to the hole in the surface and looked down into the chamber.

"Whanlaar!" he said loudly, "are you okay?!"

"Yes," Whanlaar responded. "I was surprised. I'm fine."

"Kaabar," Maalan said, "Whanlaar is fine. He landed on the floor, on his feet."

Whanlaar's voice came through the radio, "I'm in a chamber and there are suspended animation units here! I count seven of them, with our people in them.

There's an eighth one with the top open...it's empty." He rubbed the lunar dust from the glass of one chamber. "Kaabar! They seem to still be alive!"

Kaabar replied. "Is there access to the lab...can we get them out?"

"I think so. On the other side of the room there's a doorway. It looks like an entrance to the lab." He walked toward it. "Wait...Oh my God, I see a skeleton in the other room. It's on a chair in front of a big console. What do you want me to do?"

Kaabar paused a moment. "Colonel?"

Colonel Austin keyed his radio. "In everything I've read about the original rescue over 50 years ago, Mentar never mentioned that there were others in animation chambers in other locations."

Kaabar replied. "I don't think he would have known about this lab. He just worked with the students back then; he had no reason to spend time in this part of the complex. Besides, some of the archives were destroyed with the Arcology. He didn't have the information to know about them."

"Roger." Jimmy turned to his crewmembers in the suits. "Go outside, then one of you lower the other down into the lab and determine if the units are the same as the standard units the students were in." Jimmy then answered Kaabar.

"Kaabar, have your crew return to your ship. I'm sending two of my crew to check some things, so we will know what type of equipment we will need. We'll call five more guppies to come to the moon with that equipment, retrieve them, and take them to Mentar City's clinic and wake them up, there."

Kaabar acknowledged. "Apparently, one of them must have sacrificed himself to prep the others so they could survive. I want to know who he was, and I want to move his remains to the chamber where the memorial dedication is located."

"Understood," Jimmy said.

Whanlaar keyed his radio. "Kaabar, I just found a note on the Animation Control Panel, right by the skeleton. It looks like it was written in a hurry."

"Read it...in English."

Whanlaar read: *"Just alerted of the disaster...pressurizing the chambers to put my team to sleep to protect them...will get in my chamber as soon as........."*

Kaabar hesitated, "Go on, read the rest."

After a moment, Whanlaar cleared his throat. "That's all...the note wasn't finished or signed. I see a list of names on the side of the panel. The Chief Scientist is listed as Solaadar; this must be him...a leader would do this for his team. He had no idea it would happen so quickly."

Kaabar was quiet for a moment. "I remember meeting him once, at the conference where the leaders agreed to fund his animation gas research. It seems he died doing exactly what he had dreamed of doing. He deserves recognition. Get someone to help you put him in the empty chamber and seal it. When the guppy shuttles get here, we will have one take him to the

Memorial in the other tunnel. He needs a proper *Thank you.*"

"Will do, sir." After a moment he continued. "By the way, there's an open drawer under the console that appears to be full of files. Should I bring them back to the shuttle?"

"Yes, go ahead. Some of our scientists may glean some useful information from them. "

Once again, a team from NASA arrived on the moon, in full force, to recover giants from suspended animation and bring them up to the present day. Parked around the opening were six guppies, two shuttles; Colonel Austin's shuttle and a second shuttle from Cosmos that had accompanied the guppies on the transit to the Moon. Kaabar was in Mentar's personal shuttle, that had been recovered from the museum on Spaceport Zeta. All shuttle crews were now concentrating on the newly discovered mini-lab and how to recover yet seven more giants that had survived the ancient catastrophe.

The first task was to transport the remains of Solaadar to the memorial site. Kaabar and his crew accompanied the remains to the chamber and held a short ceremony to give honor to one who had given his life to save others. Kaabar would ensure that Solaadar was entered in the historical archives as a hero of the giant population.

Afterwards, the intact animation chambers were quickly separated from the gas supply, affixed with temporary supply units, and placed in the guppies for transit to Earth. The five guppies and their escort shuttles promptly departed for earth at 1G, the five-hour trajectory, to get the sleeping giants to the clinic at Mentar City. This time, when they were awakened, there would be a host of friends standing around to welcome them back to wakefulness.

Colonel Austin, in Shuttlecraft One, and Guppy 1, carrying the Moai, flew with Kaabar's party on their eleven-and-a-half-hour transit to deliver the Moai to Mentar City. When they arrived, the recovered giants would already be revived and oriented. No doubt, they would want to thank Kaabar for his memory about the Lab, and his caring.

Back, when he was still on Zannia, Kaabar had petitioned Mentar to arrange for his return to Earth on Cosmos to prepare for the end of his life. Now, he had found a new beginning instead. He called NASA, arranged for a Quantum connection to Mentar, and told him the good news of the recovery of yet another seven giant souls. He told Mentar that, initially, the seven expressed the desire to become part of the Earth colony and continue their research on both the Earth and the moon. Mentar agreed with their choice.

While descending to land at the Frank Gordon Space Flight Center and return the ship to Cosmos' hangar bay, Jimmy noticed that the Mary Lou had been moved out of the Maintenance Hangar to a parking area.

When Jimmy and crew landed in Cosmos' hangar bay, Jimmy found a message waiting, petitioning him to move Cosmos to the maintenance pad. He responded to maintenance via radio.

The chief, sporting a very positive and bubbly attitude, addressed the colonel. "Colonel, the Mary Lou's maintenance update is finished. Discovery is scheduled for maintenance next, however, before we start on her, we can work you in since you're in town."

Jimmy, smiling at the chief's demeanor, responded. "We have been hopping around the galaxy. It would be good to check her out. I'll call in the flight crew.

Bruce and Timothy moved Cosmos to the maintenance pad and shut her down. Maintenance put the ship on auxiliary power to free up the rotor pods for a complete status check and upgrades where needed.

Admiral Waddell, now retired, learning that Cosmos was in for maintenance, came to visit and view his namesake; the Waddell Cone Assembly. He visited the massive generators, then the controls and readouts. He glanced at the maintenance chief. "These giants are smart enough that they don't have to be good looking."

The chief chuckled, then took the admiral to the lounge for lunch and some conversation.

Mentar City Conference Room

The seven giants, just recently recovered from the lab on the moon, had been brought up to date on all that had happened to their world. They were astounded at the ancient destruction, the rescue of their species, especially by the *little ones*, and the return to Zannia of Mentar and his students.

The oldest of the seven survivors was especially interested in how Zannia had recovered back into a habitable planet. His name was Venataar, and he had been in the lab on the moon, researching the possible use of animation gas to control the overgrowth of hydroponic plants on extended space flights. Their plants had always tended to grow giant-sized and would continue to grow and crowd the space allotted on ships. The plants often had to be thinned and pruned to prevent the overgrowth. Venataar was trying to use the gas to possibly slow the growth when most of a ship's crew were in suspended animation, not consuming any food at all. But, his experiments had been disappointing.

During their briefings, when Venataar heard that some scientists, that had returned to Earth on Cosmos, had done a detailed study of Zannian soil, he asked to meet with them. Now, they were here in the conference room, anxious to share with the giants' leading botanical researcher. In a closed-door classified meeting, they shared their findings with the giant and expressed their concern about the SRE-17 enzyme they had brought in the soil from Zannia.

Venataar pulled out one of the files recovered from the lab on the moon. The title was, **ENZYME 'X'**. He said that he also had identified *something* in the soil causing larger growth patterns but had not had time to fully analyze it before the disaster. He revealed that Mentar City doctors had already informed him that they had noticed a lack of normal growth among most of the youth in the giant colony. They had been trying to identify some disease that might be stunting their growth.

After pouring over both sets of files, all came to the following conclusions:

Someone or *something* had intentionally *seeded* the planet Zannia with SRE-17, to ensure the large growth of its inhabitants.

The soil brought from Zannia, when it was abandoned, ensured the continued growth of the giant species.

The human colony on Zannia would eventually experience the same growth patterns as the giants.

The lack of SRE-17 in the Mentar City farm land in Kansas would result in the lack of growth among the colony residents.

After the reading of the conclusions, the scientists all looked at each other with the same question: "*Now what?*"

Venataar glanced through a second file and asked, "In your analysis on Zannia, did you notice the absence of some substance that is present in Earth's soil?"

There was a pause as the Earth scientists reviewed their work. A young intern soon raised his eyebrows with excitement. "Iodine! We didn't find iodine!"

Venataar was nodding. "Exactly…I discovered the same anomaly in the growth-pots on the moon; the absence of iodine. Evidently, SRE-17 is destroyed by iodine…without it, they can be self-replicating. Whoever seeded Zannia with the enzyme must have treated the soil with something to neutralize the iodine content. I believe that if we find a way to manipulate and control the injection of iodine into the soil, we can control the growth of populations using the soil. Experiments will confirm my theory.

If we can reintroduce iodine into the Earth colony gardens and farm land on Zannia, the colonists there will continue to experience human-level growth. Here in Mentar City, they will need help neutralizing the natural iodine content of the soil before introducing the SRE-17 samples you brought from Zannia. Then, the growth problems they are experiencing will be a thing of the past."

"Wait, Venataar," Professor Jacobson interjected, "when we isolated SRE-17 and reported it to Mentar, he expressed his feelings about disliking his size being determined by a chemical instead of nature. He ordered the scientists to develop a neutralizer to get rid of it from Zannia and let nature take over and, over time, possibly generations, determine their true size. You have determined the answer; iodine. You must communicate that to the scientists on Zannia and get it implemented. This cache of SRE-17 soil we brought with us will be destroyed. Congratulations on your research, which turns out to be even more valuable."

Venataar sat back, silent for a long time, his mind running the scenario of these developments. There was something special about returning the regulation of growth back to nature that he liked. He liked Mentar's judgement. He would contact him with his answer and travel to Zannia, to see the lush planet he had only dreamed about seeing. His scientific mind *had* to know how the planet had recovered so completely. After a Quantum Communications call and discussion with Mentar, arrangements were made for Venataar to occupy one of the giant accommodations on the next starship launched. His six fellow survivors decided to stay on Earth and research the planet that had given rise to the *little ones.*

Gordon Space Flight Center

During the ongoing days as Cosmos was going through the maintenance review, Jimmy noticed that, since Cosmos' food-producing greenhouse and hydroponics were never shut down, all the lounge areas were occupied by maintenance personnel at each mealtime. He wondered if, perhaps, that was part of the motive to service the starship.

He was glad that the service opportunity had presented itself. The chief notified him that NASA engineers had done a review of the ship because the Waddell Cone had been installed, adding considerable weight to Cosmos, namely, all six of the Waddell Cone's massive generators. NASA and the president approved the addition of twenty-five more rotor pods to the ship's drive, and five additional backups to be stored in the tool room.

Jimmy turned and looked toward Mentar City, then to the enormous mountain of scaffolding surrounding a construction pad and another soon-to-be space-worthy ship. Earlier, before Summar had launched the Quantum Cloud to return to Zylon, he had noted the near completion of an additional starship. So, he had presented to NASA another starship version of a Quantum Array to put the new ship online when her debut arrived. He also had his engineers provide the instructions for building additional arrays for future starships and for ships just designed to transit inside the solar system.

The new ship had been designed with a hundred and seventy-five rotor pods and thirty-five backups tucked away in the tool room, along with shelves full of every imaginable part for the power plant of the man-made mountain. A new space-worthy 3-D Printer was installed to enable replacement of small parts and tools when needed. That addition freed up a lot of storage room space that was usually needed for those miscellaneous parts.

Also, the ship would be staffed with peoples from around the world, who were now in dedicated training programs. Aboard would be, perhaps, two dozen of the languages that Seven could speak. However, all personnel would have a second language—English. He wondered if, when the day came that Earth's second starship parked at Spaceport Zeta, would it be the only multi-language ship to come calling.

Chapter 19

THE SCIENCE VESSEL

The Chicago Linguistics Institute contacted MIT concerning its study of the Moai found and retrieved from the moon.

The institute had been studying the extensive library found on the moon for decades. It was a rich source of information for understanding the giants. The in-depth studies were very time-consuming. Now, the focus on Saturn's moon, Iapetus, its abandonment, and the settling and development of Solaris 4, had yielded a surprise, a wild card, in the saga of the giants' occupation of the Solar System. There were records of an outside influence, after the giants had settled in on Solaris 4, that resulted in the giants building a lab complex on Solaris 4, another on the moon of Earth, and yet another on Mars.

Both the off-world labs were built into the already-existing retirement centers on those worlds. This outside influence was believed to have been in the form of Visitors from an unknown star. They were recorded as the source of the original Moai. There was a strange gap in the story flow, or information flow, in which the location and name of the home planet of those Visitors was lost. It's context, as suggested by the experts at the Institute, seemed to indicate a coverup. Why? A hint came from the fact that, the very next recorded study was when the giants, the Zannians, began genetic experiments with the great apes of Earth, resulting in early man coming to be. There were many comparative studies done and then, finally, summing up the finds by the various groups, the scientists dropped a bombshell. Their report read…

> *"The genetic material that had resulted in the rise of humans, also produced the giants.* ***The giants did not use their own genetic material to cause the rise of humans, but a borrowed one.*** *It was suspected to be present in the amber fluid discovered on the moon in the water-heater-sized bottles, the ones discovered near the giants that had survived. The bottles had been taken to Earth and the amber fluid subsequently studied at length. There were several unidentifiable chemicals in the solution, two of which evaporated in a matter of minutes when exposed to the air. After extensive study, no definitive conclusions were reached."*

Now, the search for *who we really are and where we really came from* became the focus of planet Earth's scientists. Once the scientists came by that tidbit of information, they would not let it go. Up until this revelation, they were just *little ones* mixed up in a test tube by the giants. However, now, they were the giant's equals. They were somebody and that felt good.

They must have that validated. The heavy names and reputations of the planet-wide scientific community began petitioning their various governments for a dedicated mission to find that planet and determine conclusively where the Zannians and humans actually originated. Thus, soon, the heads of state across the planet would collectively cut the ribbon on a brand-new starship, that had been under construction for years. With just a few modifications, it was transformed into a science vessel...the **OMNI-STAR.**

The scientific community interpreted the meaning of the ship's name, using a Latin slant, as *a vessel to seek out knowledge among the stars.* All space-faring nations had contributed to the funding of the vessel and the construction thereof. Collectively, all nations would be represented on board the Omni-Star, and all petitioned that the seasoned commander and crew of Cosmos fly her. Colonel Austin and crew's next mission was already on the books, without a destination.

The backup crew of Cosmos moved into her center seat. The third string of Cosmos moved to the backup position aboard the Omni-Star.

Captains Snyder and Abbott and crews would fly the DOEs out of Cosmos and into the Omni-Star. The Air Force built new ones, to replace the DOEs on Cosmos; citing the valuable contributions of their predecessors. All DOEs and shuttles were equipped with Quantum Array antennas.

The Linguistics Institute's meeting with MIT was scheduled to take place in NASA's conference room in Houston.

MIT had done extensive studies on the Moai with delicate measuring comparisons with the copies on Easter Island. The laser work of the giants was good, however, there were differences. The Moai on Easter Island all matched each other, all made of volcanic rock. The Moai from the lunar Arcology was unique— different. The most important piece of information was the spectrum-analysis of the material of the statue itself. There was no match on planet Earth. It was not built here. However, that was already believed by circumstantial evidence. This original Moai had arrived on the moon long ago. The hot question was: Just where did it come from.

The Quantum Array enabled MIT to contact Zannia and request they check the Moai found in the Zolaadine mines, now located at the Zannian spaceport. They did so and experienced the same results; no match on Zannia. Also, it was determined by the analysis that the Zannian statue and the Lunar statue were identical.

Colonel Austin and his team suggested that the first stop in the Omni-Star's search should be the library at Spaceport Zeta. The scientists had already been planning for such a venture. The Captain's Daily Log, aboard Cosmos, all during her journeys, had dutifully been transmitted to NASA, outlining her travels. The scientific community had reviewed Cosmos' Log and discovered the existence of the library. Perhaps there were records of the Moai there, and, just maybe, the Moai's home address.

DAN HOLT and MAX HOLT

Chapter 20

THE OMNI-STAR

Something magical happened when the news of the discovery spread around the planet. The giants were not indeed our makers, but our brothers and sisters in the grand scheme of things. We were both made from the same mold, the spiritual mold of sentience, but of slightly different sizes. Our varied skin-tones as peoples were touches added by the giants; just because they could. An act that set aside planet Earth as unique.

The deep, demanding thirst to know, surfaced and must be appeased. Who are we, really; where did we come from? What is our true origin? Who or what is responsible? We are here. We are aware. Why can't we know our cradle?

Once again, the scaffolding, rigging, molds, equipment, and thousands of tools had been cleared away from a shiny new starship. The Omni-Star was put through all the rigorous testing to ascertain space worthiness. Now, she stood there on the launching pad; a promise. She would represent the entire planet and fly, with purpose, to answer the question that lives in the hearts of the peoples of Earth.

Finally, Jimmy stood on the Bridge of the Omni-Star, gleaming with newness. For weeks he had been *personalizing* the new ship, making it *his own*. He was gazing at the framed photo he had just had installed behind the Captain's Chair; a photo of what had gotten this incredible adventure started. As he smiled, smiling back at him was the original ship, Research One, and her amazing crew. When his communicator rang, he answered it without losing his gaze on the photo.

"Colonel Austin."

"Colonel, this is Pearson with Starship Engineering. Your new personal shuttle is finished and ready for delivery to the Omni-Star, but we have one problem."

"I've got to have that shuttle onboard by tomorrow, to allow time to program the computer systems. What's the problem?"

"The name, sir…we don't have the name to paint on the outside. What name shall we give it?

Still staring at the photo, imagining the *unknowns* he was about to experience, Jimmy smiled. "Research Two…she will be called Research Two."

The compliment of Cosmos had returned to earth; changed. They could no longer envision a separated and fragmented planet. It was so childish, ludicrous, and wasteful. The dispersal of the groups of early man by the giants, no doubt in ignorance, had created the separatism of the growing sentient beings. It could be fixed. It would take a great deal of time, but it could be fixed. The upcoming venture would be a perfect initiative. Different peoples, a common goal, and need.

In the process of continuing mission preparations, Colonel Austin and his bridge crew once again walked up the ramp of the starship and headed for the bridge. Stepping up onto the bridge floor, they walked along the console and looked at the new appointments. The layout of the readouts, controls, and gauges were the same, except for the Rotor Pod Status display. It was larger. It now included twenty-five additional rotor pods, totaling 175, now powering the ship.

The designers of the ship had planned ahead for future *special guests* who may be onboard; they had constructed five living spaces, designed for giant-sized passengers. So, if Jimmy needed the assistance of Zannians or Zylonians, the ship was ready to accommodate.

Timothy Dalton, copilot, looked up from the console. "Colonel, the weight of our starships has grown due to beneficial additions. I'm wondering if maybe we should look at developing larger rotor pods with more power, so we wouldn't need so many."

"Good point, Tim. However, I like the use of multiple pods because if one is damaged or simply quits working for some reason, the effect is minimal. There are records of the early days of spaceship Discovery, on its way to Mars, when it was hit by an incredibly dense small projectile that took out one of the rotor pods. There was no loss of acceleration because of the design of multiple rotor pods. If we had larger ones, say, a dozen, and one quit, the difference in available power would be of a concern."

"I see what you mean, sir. In fact, if you think about it, the whole bottom deck of the ship, the engine room, is the power plant of the ship."

"There's one other thing," Jimmy added, "I trust them to take care of this ship. I walk down those stairs from time to time just to hear them humming. Dolan probably thinks I'm checking on him."

"I don't think so, Colonel; he knows the magic. He claims that they are all singing, in the key of **D**."

Bruce Wilson, now the Omni-Star's pilot, sat down in the center seat and placed his hand on the control stick. It felt new. He moved it through its range of motion. The scene of steering Cosmos through the entrance port of Spaceport Zeta flowed across his mind. A half-mile wide behemoth obeying a six-inch-long control. The feeling of controlling such mass and power was indescribable. Here, this baby was even more powerful, with its engine room additions, and more purposeful. She would be representing all of Earth. He wanted to return to Spaceport Zeta, and so wanted all the new people who would be on board to see it. And, just maybe, the day would come when he would have the privilege of steering the Omni-Star into a wormhole and have her travel light-years in days instead of years; the true realization of conquering the stars.

The crew could hear the occasional sounds coming from the parts of the ship where dozens of technicians were setting up the greenhouse and hydroponics areas. Many of the vegetables that had been planted while the Omni-Star was being constructed, were being transplanted on board. It was an enormous undertaking and would be permanent when the Hydroponic Section was fully functional as were all the galleys on the ships. There was an Earth fleet now, of respectable size. It included the Omni-Star, Cosmos, Discovery, the two space cargo ships, the Maxie Gene and the Mary Lou, along with dozens of smaller craft, without galleys but with ration storage instead. They were all designated for government use and were maintained at the Frank Gordon Spaceport.

Jimmy and crew boarded two R-bots and began a three-mile tour of the main floor, circumnavigating it. Just past the main entrance ramp, a hundred feet wide, was a line of research labs, a dozen of them. Ten of them were specifically stocked as per the science group designated to use them, and then a linguistics lab, and a general research lab. They were equipped with research tools and appliances as designated by the various countries that would be using them as the Omni-Star searched the expansive area of the galaxy for answers.

Past those, there was an enormous meeting room, or convention center for the same use. These various scientific groups would gradually blend together, and work to unravel the mysteries of space. They would need lots of brainstorming room.

Aboard the Omni-Star would be 120 scientists, great minds, filled with a burning desire to know the universe. From its concentration and distribution of noble gasses, its complicated dispersion of gravity wells; some so powerful that they bend light rays, the how and why of its black holes, and most important, the science of wormholes and how they are traveled.

Touring the labs, while the construction crews concluded the final check of the ship's completion, the bridge crew was awed at the various equipment included in the science labs of the different groups of scientists.

Bruce Wilson, pilot, admiring the lab equipment, turned to the colonel. "There are 120 of these guys. Do you think the addition of 25 rotor pods is going to be enough the get this much intellect off the ground?"

Colonel Austin smiled. "I think a bigger issue may be getting these guys to come back home. Just think, they have spent much of a career learning what is possible to learn while grounded on Earth. Now, they are finally getting a chance to go where the science is; where it's happening."

Farther on, the lounge and the giant porthole looked inviting. Upon looking at the porthole, all eyes automatically went to the top center of the ship. The giant eye, the window, was mesmerizing. As the tour continued, the quarters were pristine and new and roomy and inviting. The ship was a beautiful place where one could spend the rest of his life and never feel bored or empty. No doubt, this crew would do just that, occasionally touching base back home.

As the Omni-Star approached readiness, the scientists began arriving. There were groups of 12 each, from the US, Russia, China, and India, then 6 each from Australia, Japan, Mexico, and Canada. Then, by committees in the nation groups, 12 each were chosen from the European, the South American, African, and Middle Eastern nations.

A hundred and twenty of Earth's best minds. There was electricity in the air as they began to interact. They got little sleep. There was so much they wanted to share about their various goals and this god-send of an opportunity. The authorities bantered: "We are going to have to get these people off the ground, so they can get some sleep." However, it was admitted that the labs aboard, with the latest of everything, would only make it worse. It was the greatest gathering of scientific minds since Apollo.

And yet, there was more. A decision was made to equip a research area for graduate students in the field of Astronomy; two each from twenty-five of the major Universities around the planet. They would have a golden opportunity to be understudies, in a closed environment, of the top minds of planet Earth. The Observatory Modules of Omni-Star had telescopes ten times more powerful than the ancient Hubble Telescope that had circled the Earth for so many years. The students' scholastic discipline was about the stars; they were going to take a closer look.

The powers that be also designated a special area and necessary supplies for writers and historians to be on board and record all the Omni-Star's exploits in the Literary Data Base of the ship's computer system. They even had the supplies to create printed pages, if necessary, for posterity. The library would be a treasure trove upon the Omni-Star's return to her home world. Especially if within her many documents was the answer to the question that launched the science vessel...the birthplace of mankind.

Chapter 21

QUANTUM COMMUNICATIONS

The call came from the direction of Bernard's Star. The Quantum Equipment in NASA's communications building activated and a circle of lights around a black mushroom button began pulsing, accompanied by an electronic gong; something like the sound accompanying the opening of an elevator door. A screen, displaying an array of star charts in a spherical hologram that encased the Solar System, scrolled to a point where Bernard's Star was in the center of the screen.

Jacob Watkins, a clerk, temporarily manning Communications at NASA's newly installed Quantum equipment, looked from the display to a fellow files clerk? "What do I say? That's somebody calling from another star."

"Try, hello."

Jacob looked at the assistant, then blinked. "Maybe I am taking this too seriously." He stepped over to the equipment, then pushed the button. "Hello, this is Earth."

There was a moment of silence, then: *"This is Summar, from Zylon, aboard the Quantum Cloud, I request communication with Colonel Jimmy Austin, Commander, Cosmos. I attempted a direct link to his ship, but it was unsuccessful."*

"Yes. He's not here at the moment. He's aboard the Omni-Star, our new starship, a science vessel, getting it ready to launch. The Quantum equipment hasn't been installed on it yet. I can have him call you back."

"Understood."

The equipment went dark. Jacob looked around at his buddy. "They don't mince words, do they."

"He's speaking through a translating device."

"Oh, yeah, he is, isn't he."

"And receiving you through it. Jacob, you just talked on the phone star to star."

"Yeah, I did, didn't I."

After receiving the message, Colonel Austin boarded Cosmos and went directly to the communications department. The skeleton staff of one technician was studying one of the tech manuals on the Quantum equipment. He looked up. Jimmy glanced at him then seated himself in the Comm-chair. "Walter, get me the code for the Quantum Cloud. I need to call Summar."

"Yes, sir," he said, his fingers flowing over the keyboard of the new equipment. "Shall I initiate the call?"

"Yes, go ahead."

Moments later the equipment came alive, located the source of the transmission, then the sounds of Summar's translator filled the communications room. *"This is Summar, aboard the Quantum Cloud. Colonel Austin—Cosmos?"*

"Yes, Summar, I'm here.

"Colonel, I called you on your main equipment base in your headquarters and your starship because it will record this call. Your personal device, your communicator will not."

"Why does this call need to be recorded?" Jimmy asked.

"For the records at Spaceport Zeta. I received a call from Tholan. Spaceport Zeta would like detailed information about your planet Earth for the library records of the Spaceport. There's already been multiple requests for information about you. They also have requested information from Zannia."

"Yes, I know. I talked to Mentar earlier. "Okay," Jimmy continued, "I'll talk to the heads of State and get them to put together a cache of records describing our planet. It's going to take some time. We have many varied peoples here on Earth."

"That's the most requested information concerning your planet."

"Soon, we will be taking over a hundred of our scientists to Spaceport Zeta to make use of her library. At that time, they can provide the records you desire."

"Excellent, Colonel. Let me know when you launch for the Spaceport. I must see your new ship."

"Will do, Summar. Goodbye for now," Jimmy said and terminated the connections.

Jimmy petitioned Walter to contact Mentar on Zannia. He answered promptly.

"Go ahead, Colonel," Mentar said.

"Mentar, when do you plan to visit Spaceport Zeta? We are putting the Omni-Star into service in about two months. I'd like to meet you there."

"We can coordinate with that," Mentar said. "We are preparing Little One and selecting the young scientists that will board the ship for an educational tour of the space station."

"Great, my friend," Jimmy said. "Mentar, don't forget…delegate…delegate, get plenty of rest."

"Work is a hard habit to break, but, I have already started the process for the younger to take over much of these responsibilities."

"Good, I'll look forward to seeing you at Zeta. I hope you got the word about the passenger and the supplies we are transporting for Little One City on Zannia. We have about 20 tons of supplies and equipment for them, and one school teacher. Also Venentaar will be aboard."

"Yeah, I know. "I'm looking forward to finally meeting him."

"I would appreciate it if you could transfer them and the cargo to your ship at Zeta and deliver them for us. That would help keep us on our research vigil."

"Yes, Colonel. I will be glad to help my old friend. After all, you seem to want a date with the stars. I hope you and your crew will be ready for what you might find at the end of your quest."

"We hope so too. Just let me know your expected arrival date and I will adjust our velocity appropriately."

"Roger…will do."

Chapter 22

THE FIRST OFFICER

The sun peeped over the horizon, highlighting the Omni-Star. Jimmy contemplated its profile for a long moment. The adventure ahead, the first mission of the new vessel, would, no doubt, be the peak of his career. Seeking the origin of mankind; the cradle; the start of it all. To know that answer.

The science vessel sported seventeen excursion craft. Six shuttles, six guppies, the commander's, Colonel Austin's personal shuttle, the two DOEs, and, a new creation by the engineers, the two Quadro-pods. They were new excursion craft based on the guppy's design, but with twice the power. The engineers beefed up the frame of the craft, then added two additional rotor pods, four in all, thus; the designation: Quadro-pods; Quad 1 and Quad 2. The vehicle, in a dire emergency, could actually tow the mother ship; the Omni-Star.

NASA, the bridge crew of the Omni-Star, the captains and crews of the two DOEs, the President and his advisors, and a team of nuclear technicians, met and conducted a review of the history of the DOEs since they had been assigned to duty on Cosmos. The special ships had performed magnificently when called upon in several situations. However, in view of their current duty, it was determined that they were excessively armed. The authorities decided to remove the multiple warhead missiles and replace them with simple low yield neutron torpedoes, capable of destroying an offending asteroid or comet. It would best serve the Omni-Star. The laser cannons, that had proved to be so beneficial, would remain.

Colonel Jimmy Austin was up early looking forward to today's business. A first officer, to back up Jimmy himself, would be formally installed into the staff of the science vessel. After several hours-long sessions with Jimmy, NASA, and the president's staff, Bruce Wilson, the current pilot of the Omni-Star, was chosen as the First Officer. His backup would be moved into the front-most position with the bridge crew and the second backup to the first backup position.

Then, the committee chose the first backup pilot of Discovery to move to the science vessel as the third backup. The appointee, Harley Trellis, relished the development of being assigned to the Omni-Star, a move from interplanetary to interstellar duty, and looked forward to sailing the seas of space. He would get plenty of hands on duty. Sailing the heavens is an around-the-clock business.

The ceremony was brief. The President outlined the qualifications and the duties of the new official position of backing up the current commander of the starship, Colonel Austin. Bruce officially accepted the position and pledged his best efforts on behalf of the President and the nation. And so, the Omni-Star had a first officer, capable, respected by all, and seasoned. Sheldon Darcy, Bruce's 1st backup, also seasoned at the helm, assumed the pilot's position.

DAN HOLT and MAX HOLT

Chapter 23

LAUNCH

The Omni-Star, carefully prepped for a likely ten-year mission, sat in its majesty on the tarmac of the Frank Gordon Space Flight Center. The greatest gathering of heads-of-state was in progress as they who represented the various countries involved in the creation and financing of the science vessel attended to tour the ship and wish their scientists well.

Network cameras were everywhere with hundreds of interviews going on with the travelers and their families that would stay at home. Many personal stories were being lived, stories that would surface later as special memories.

News organizations world-wide couldn't get enough of three special stories associated with this historic mission.

First, was the impending departure of Venataar, soon to be the chief botanical researcher on Zannia. His survival from the ancient disaster and recovery in the moon lab made him the one interviewee that was sure to double media ratings.

As the only Human Earthling permanently moving to Zannia on this trip, Lilah Owenby was popular on all news channels. Since she would become the Headmaster of the growing school system for the Zannian colonists, the U.S. Minister of Education designated her as the **Teacher to the Stars** and awarded her the first honorary doctorate in Off-Planet Education. She would not disappoint her family or her planet. She would be blazing the trail for many more to follow her in the future.

Another one, garnering high media ratings, was Amil Lajahda, from India. He was born in a tent city at a missionary camp sponsored by Great Britain. Raised in poverty, always gazing at the stars, he, through great sacrifice by his parents and the help of the British missionary, managed to go through college. He was now a graduate student in astronomy and chosen to fly on the Omni-Star. Standing at the base of the entrance ramp of the starship embracing his mother, he leaned down close to her ear and whispered: "I'm going to bring you something from the stars."

Thousands were gathered around while the designated crews and compliment of the ship were saying their goodbyes and boarding the starship. Upon the final closing of the ramp and the powering up for launch of the starship, there were 942 souls aboard the Omni-Star. The First Officer gave his first command and she rose from the Space Flight Center to begin a search among the stars. First stop; Spaceport Zeta.

The Omni-Star was just clearing the cloud level in the central Kansas skies when Colonel Austin gave an all-stop order. Bruce Wilson, the first officer, quickly brought the starship to Station-Keeping, hovering at 30,000 feet. Colonel Austin addressed Bruce.

"Dispatch a guppy to Easter Island and pick up a Moai and bring it to the Omni-Star. Mentar wants to donate it to the museum at Spaceport Zeta." He had contacted NASA about it the day before; they contacted the authorities on the Island and made the arrangements. "They have picked it out," he said. "It's waiting for you to pick up."

The crew of Guppy 1 quickly powered up their ship, exited the hangar bay and headed for the Island. Kaabar, petitioned by NASA, had already ferried four of the colonists, the giants, to load the treasure. Although a duplicate, it did represent the real thing. Perhaps, when the source planet was found and visited, there would be the real thing available to replace this copy at Zeta.

The giants were delighted and honored to load the gift in the guppy for shipment to Zeta to be displayed there for all to see. The guppy returned to the Omni-Star with the treasure, then the starship resumed its mission to find...man.

DAN HOLT and MAX HOLT

Chapter 24

THE MAIDEN VOYAGE

Most on Earth were watching the Giants' Channel as the Omni-Star disappeared toward the outer planets. As they passed Neptune's orbital plane and entered the Kuiper Belt, with the wormhole vortex, Jimmy wished his crew had already had the training to access the *tunnel* that would save incredible amounts of time while traversing space. The Onmi-Star was ready, but the crew would have to wait until they could get their training at Zeta. Perhaps...on the way back home, sometime in the future.

The Omni-Star left the solar system behind and lined up on the coordinates for Spaceport Zeta. The scientists watched the solar system recede to become points of light like the many surrounding it. The Waddell Cone was engaged, and the starship became a projectile, exempt from collision, traversing the distance it must travel with greatly reduced time.

The scientists referred often to their courtesy monitors in their respective labs; monitors for viewing, live, fore and aft of the Omni-Star. There was, thoughtfully, large monitors included in the conference room; soon to become a lecture hall. Two of the enterprising young scientists, one from the US and one from Russia, recognizing the vast pool of knowledge of the various scientific disciplines, began petitioning and scheduling various lectures on the many disciplines aboard. Venataar was called upon many times to discuss his work as the head botanist for the giants. Of special interest was his work with the animation gas experiments. All the learned, now sailing among the stars, were eager to learn and express themselves.

The 'lecture hall' was filled with scientists daily, each enjoying their time spent with their dedicated colleagues. Colonel Austin scheduled himself to attend one of the lectures. That day's offering was: **Quasars—Markers of the Universe**. A scientist from England took the podium and began. In about fifteen minutes, Jimmy got full. He politely excused himself to 'go check on the bridge'.

Zannia

Menvaar Ataar Kievanne, the son of Mentar was assigned to head the government during Mentar's and Kronos's absence. The young statesman had proven himself to have sound judgement regarding matters of state. Approved by the people, he served on the advisory board to the planet's leader.

Kronos had petitioned to be included on the visit to the Zeta spaceport. Starship Little One was prepped for the journey and the 100 scientists and students boarded her. She launched the same day as the Omni-Star. Arrival of the two vessels would be within days of each other.

In the cargo hold of Little One was Zolaadine Man. The ancient robot was not aboard to be presented to the museum, but, instead, to be researched to see if there was any information in the library regarding him; who he was, when he was, and why he was. The dating of the rock strata in which he was found indicated that he had been disabled and left there over a half-million years earlier. That would be well before the giants abandoned Zannia; before Zannia was in ecological trouble. If the giant species had even emerged at the time, it would have been in their infancy.

Mentar wondered if Zannia was visited by others planning to lay claim on the planet, who then encountered others with the same plans. A bitter battle could have ensued, perhaps a battle so devastating that neither side was capable of claiming anything. Maybe, somewhere in the bulbous records of the Zeta library, there were some answers. The group that had unearthed the mystery was aboard and filled with anticipation.

Bernard's Star – Zylon 2

Summar, having received notice when the Omni-Star would launch, gave the order to launch the Quantum Cloud. She was loaded with an additional stock of Communications Arrays for storage on Spaceport Zeta, and other various types of equipment and replacement parts for maintenance of the space station. Summar, intrigued by the Earth people, timed his dutiful visit to the spaceport to coincide with their arrival.

Aboard the Omni-Star

With the Omni-Star well on her way to Spaceport Zeta, Colonel Austin and his first officer, Bruce Wilson, began a walking tour of the starship; a vigil that would take a week, therefore was spread over the first month of the flight. Today, they headed for the engine room.

"Mr. Darcy, you have the bridge," Bruce said, then he and Jimmy headed for the stairs leading to the engine room.

Chief Matthew Dolan was sitting in his office making an entry on his computer terminal. He looked up through his office window and saw the colonel and first officer reaching the bottom of the stairs. He stood, came out of the office and met them. Colonel Austin sniffed the air then looked at the Chief. "There's a faint scent in the air. What is that?"

The Chief smiled. "That's a low viscosity oil coating on the rotor pods that's been warmed up and kept warm. When the rotor pods were fabricated, tested, and certified, they were coated in the special oil to prevent deterioration while in storage. The smell will be gone in a few days."

Bruce's eyes swept the half-mile diameter sea of spheres, each eight-foot in diameter, spread evenly across the entire engine room. There were nine gaps in the spread. It appeared that a pod was missing where there should have been one. He turned to the Chief. "There are nine empty spots on the floor."

"Yes, sir. That's where the nine landing struts come up into the cabin. You can see them on the tour." The Chief indicated a blue line with arrows that meandered through the rotor pods. "The blue line that you see there marks a route through the engine room that takes you within a visual and ear-shot of all the running rotor pods. Two of my staff walk it twice a day to check on the rotor pods, first hand."

"Sounds like they are all running smoothly," Bruce said.

"Yes, sir. My 175 angels will carry this ship to the stars."

Jimmy smiled. "Mr. Dolan, you are a romantic."

"Yes, sir."

Jimmy looked again across the sea of rotor pods, then his eyes came to rest on the fifty-foot diameter column in the center of the engine room. "Chief, let's board your R-bot. Take us out to that column, I want to get a closer look at that telescope."

"Yeah, that was a great addition; Cosmos didn't have that."

Jimmy nodded, "The scientists requested it; makes sense, this *is* a science vessel."

Chief Dolan parked the R-bot next to one of the view ports in the column. The three men gathered around it and peered inside. There was a short-barreled telescope, ten meters in diameter, mounted with servomotors and electronics for tracking and to transmit the 'seeing' to the Observatory Lab on Deck 4. When used, a port would open on the bottom of the ship. The column in the engine room sealed the telescope outside in space, and the environment of the ship inside.

The Chief returned his visitors to the foot of the stairs.

"Thank you, Chief," Jimmy said.

"Yes, sir, you're welcome."

Jimmy and Bruce headed back up the stairs. Bruce glanced at Jimmy. "That guy makes me feel comfortable about this engine room."

"Yeah, me too. Did you know that he can tell you if a rotor pod is in order by listening to it; the pitch of its humming sound."

"Really?"

"Yeah, it's amazing. He trained the Sheldon kid that we took to Zannia with the colonists.

"Sheldon kid?"

"You remember…the tomato thief."

"Oh, yeah. I remember him. When I heard about it, it made my mouth water. I wanted a tomato."

"Did you get one?"

"No, sir."

At the top of the stairs, Jimmy turned toward the elevators. "Let's take a look at Deck 4; the animation units and the Observatory."

Both men had walked through the deck before, as they had all the decks during the construction process.

But, with so many decks and so much space on each, it was only in passing. This 'tour' was to see any details that might be significant. They stepped off the elevator and entered the deck. The spread of animation units, 1000 on the science vessel, versus 2000 on Cosmos, seemed overwhelming, despite there being half as many as on the previous starship in which they had sailed the heavens.

The Omni-Star was designed for a maximum compliment of 1000, as much of her space was taken up by science instruments. Since the animation units occupied less than half of the dedicated deck, the remainder of the floor space was cordoned off for a science lab...the Observatory; pursuing the science of astronomy.

There were four large monitors spread along the wall of the ship, all accompanied by desks, laden with computers, and tables and chairs. There were at least forty of the scientists in the lab. They were gathered in groups in discussion, some on the computers, and several pointing out objects on the monitors; of which all four were busy.

The telescopes, both fore and aft, were on line. Mounted in the top of the Omni-Star, a hundred feet from the center porthole, opposite the windshield, was a duplicate of the telescope arrangement in the engine room. The graduate students, and the seasoned scientists had expressed a desire to study the solar system as it dropped away behind the starship. They arranged files, ready to receive their observations of the Oort Cloud, the Kuiper Belt, the Heliopause, and the Bow Shock, around the star they call home. This being the first time they were given the 'gift' of seeing them from afar.

Upon exiting the deck, Jimmy and Bruce paused just briefly and looked at animation units #1 and #2, their assigned places to pass the time—and the seemly endless miles.

They checked on the bridge, then headed for the aft lounge and lunch. The waiter appeared. He was wearing a lapel pin. It was two figurines mounted on a two-inch circular background. One was flexed in an Atlas stance; the other standing beside him, looking up at him. His height reached to about the larger figure's knee. The caption read: *I'm a giant fan.* Jimmy's eyes went from the lapel to the waiter's face.

"I bought it at Giant City, ah, I mean Mentar City."

Jimmy smiled and nodded. then glanced at Bruce. "What are you having?"

"Potato soup with Cauliflower Bread, and a tomato on the side."

Jimmy laughed. "Make that two."

Chapter 25

STARMAN

Colonel Austin arose early, an ingrained habit, and headed for the bridge for his usual heads-up on the status of the ship. Upon arrival, he was given the update; all was nominal. Then Melvin, just going on duty, looked at a note left for him by the shift just relieved. It read:

The Astronomers on Deck 4 want to see the Colonel when he arrives at the bridge in the morning. It seems that they have spotted something close to the solar system.

Melvin looked around, spotted the colonel: "Colonel, a note for you," he said and handed Jimmy the note from Deck 4.

Jimmy read it, then headed for the elevators.

When the astronomers saw him approaching from the elevator, they pulled a photo out of their storage bin.

"Colonel," the team leader began, "we spotted this asteroid closing on the solar system." He was pointing at a faint spot of light on the photograph, a copy, of an image from the aft telescope. "We tracked it through the night. It's still about a year and a half from the solar system, but our numbers show that it's going to make a very close pass by Mars orbit. There could be an impact."

"We are in the process of rebuilding that planet," Jimmy said. "We don't need an impact. How big is it?"

"It's very difficult to size it at this distance."

"How far are we from the solar system?"

"Well, Colonel, to put it in perspective, do you have a quarter in your pocket?"

Jimmy raised his eyebrows, then reached into his pocket and took out a quarter and held it up.

"Hold it at arm's length," the lead astronomer said.'

Jimmy complied. "Now," the astronomer continued, "Turn it sideways just a little. That's the orbit of Pluto from where you are now. Our best estimate of the object's size is between a quarter and a half-mile in diameter. Could we send the DOEs to kill it, ah, pulverize it?"

"We'll radio NASA to take care of it. They can send Cosmos to meet it. They will need the coordinates— it's location, from you."

Jimmy and the team leader headed for communications to raise NASA and inform them of the threat. Jimmy looked at the tall gangly scientist. "What's your name?"

"My grandchildren call me Starman," the astronomer responded, 'but it's Howard Wiggins."

"Well, Starman," Jimmy responded in a positive manner, "you guys have done a great thing here. Not too many years ago, we had to take our chances on being in the cross hairs of a comet or asteroid."

"Colonel, it's my job. Being on this ship is the top of my life."

DAN HOLT and MAX HOLT

Chapter 26

THE WRECKAGE

The Omni-Star sailed on in the sea of space. The scientists were engrossed in their equipment, probing the surrounding space on the freeway to the spaceport. None, on this first trek of the mission, wanted to make use of the animation units and pass the time. They wanted to spend every waking moment studying their surroundings; unique surroundings provided by a starship sailing through the heavens.

Jimmy set up the appropriate crew rotations for fair time distributions on duty. Many, on an interstellar vessel for the first time, wanted to remain awake and aware. Their request was honored. Jimmy went to his unit, set his timer for eight months, and suspended his awareness and his aging; any incident, it would be returned immediately as per his standing orders. His first officer had the bridge.

Bruce Wilson sat in the command chair. His gaze slowly swept the 150 feet wide and 150 feet high windshield of the Omni-Star. He was in control of a half-mile wide, powerful machine. His mind went back to the first machine that had gotten him off the ground. He pictured the ancient J-3 Cub, a two-passenger, high wing, 65 horsepower flying machine, and imagined it, sitting on the floor of the main deck of the Omni-Star.

Now, it would look like a toy, lost in the expanse of the half-mile wide starship. His first solo flight could have taken place on the main deck of the Omni-Star. He imagined the crewmembers walking around it, looking it over in amusement; maybe reaching up, grasping the end of the wind and shaking it just to believe it was there and really had a wing. However, there was a time when it was an awesome machine. It would fly.

Speaking of flight; they were about to enter the fascinating world of wormhole travel. Bruce knew it was serious business. However, he had read Katy's report on her encounter/interview with the Lindian doctor at the Aisle Side Lounge. To that advanced civilization, wormhole travel was routine.

When they arrived at Spaceport Zeta, while the scientists are combing through the library for information on the Moai, he would petition Seven for a seminar on wormhole travel. With the colonel's approval, which he knew would be forthcoming, he would arrange for all three bridge crews, himself, and the Colonel, to be completely briefed on the phenomenon. To be able to travel to, say, the Pleiades, over 400 light-years, in just over a year, would be fantastic. The rest of the mission time would be from their starting place to the vortex, and then, from vortex to destination.

"If and when," Bruce thought, "we get involved in wormhole travel, I would want Seven, or one of his colleagues with us; at least the first time. He would have to check with the Stationmaster, Tholan, and see if one could rent an android." Bruce smiled at himself.

Summar's engineers had told him on Earth that the Omni-Star was sturdy enough to be wormhole capable.

"Look at that!" came from his bridge crew, bringing Bruce's mind back to the moment.

"What have we got?"

"Sir," Sharon, safety officer, responded. "There's a ship up ahead. It's about half a million miles out and roughly two hundred miles starboard."

"At that distance, how do you know it's a ship?"

"It's transmitting a repeating signal, maybe a distress call."

Bruce sat straight up in his seat. "All stop, all stop." Bruce keyed the intercom again. "Deck 4, wake the Colonel."

Minutes later, Colonel Austin approached the bridge, taking deep breaths and rotating his shoulders and neck. Bruce relinquished the command chair, then filled in the Colonel of the discovery.

"It's in the far outer ring of the Oort Cloud," Jimmy said, "did it collide with something?"

"Don't know, sir; we're getting a constant signal, a code, that keeps repeating. Perhaps it's an automatic distress call."

"Pipe it through to the science lab and get them to work on it. We need to know what it is saying as quickly as they can."

The Omni-Star, as per instructions from the bridge, after sounding the alarm, disengaged the Waddell

Cone. With the fabric of space unwrapped from the vessel, Jimmy called for a reversal of the ship, so it could began decelerating.

Jimmy keyed the intercom. "All personnel, we are in process of checking on a starship that's adrift up ahead. Be prepared for weightlessness to last for a short time, possibly hours."

"Colonel," Sharon reported, "we are going to bypass the vessel by about two thousand miles before we reach zero velocity."

"Not too bad," Jimmy said. "As soon as we are stopped, steer back to it and let's see what's happened there." Jimmy keyed the intercom again. "Captains Snyder and Abbott, to the bridge."

"We've been monitoring, sir," came from the intercom. "We're on our way."

Abbott glanced at Snyder. "I hope this is not **Battle beyond the Stars**," then grinned.

"You read that book, too?"

"When I was a kid," Abbott said. "When I learned, in school, about Mr. Gordon building that first flying saucer, I wanted to fly it. I would lie awake at night and think about flying it around the moon, looking for giants, then flying back to Earth. I read all the books I could find about space."

"It's not surprising that you are aboard the Omni-Star."

Jimmy turned to the arriving DOE pilots. "When we arrive at the vessel, launch and standby. We'll pull up alongside and launch a shuttle. First, we'll try to get a response from inside. If there's no radio response, we may have to just knock on the hull, and check the portholes, etc. If there's none. We'll attempt to gain entry and send in two crewmembers. Perhaps you should have a couple of your crew suited and ready just in case.

"Yes, sir," Snyder said, then he and Abbott went to assemble their crews and prep their ships.

When the Omni-Star came to Station-Keeping, Sheldon Stacy, pilot, locked the radar onto the drifting vessel and engaged power to intercept. His equipment showed it to be 2,171 miles away. Stacy set 1G acceleration for 1,000 miles, then auto-deceleration for the second 1,000.

The ship loomed ahead. As the Omni-Star approached, the crew engaged inertial braking, slowly moving to a hundred feet separation between the vessels. The cigar-shaped craft, about a thousand feet long and two hundred in diameter, black in color, was tumbling slowly end over end. It was making one revolution about every five or six minutes.

Colonel Austin ordered the three excursion ships launched. "Captain Snyder, can you use your DOE to stop the rotation?"

"I think so, sir. I can fly to the center of the ship, approach to within a couple of feet of it, then follow the hull out to the end on the accelerating side then land on it and apply gentle pressure."

"Okay. Take your time, not too much pressure: we don't know how old that hull is, or how strong."

"Yes, sir. Approaching the ship." Snyder eased his craft toward the center of mass. When he closed to ten feet, he matched the rotation with his craft, then flew to the rotation side, placing his ship in the rotation path. He looked to his left, to the side of the ship that was hidden from the Omni-Star.

"Colonel," he said hastily, "the ship has been breached. There's a huge hole ripped in the side of it. It's about forty or fifty feet long and five or six feet wide. There can't be anybody alive, unless they were already in suits or in suspended animation before this happened. This rupture would decompress this ship in seconds. It must have been hit by something high speed and sizable."

Jimmy and crew were quiet for a moment. "Captain," Jimmy said, "go ahead and stop the rotation, then we'll move the Omni-Star to that side of the ship for a visual from the bridge, then enter the vessel and check it out."

The bridge crew watched the skilled, seasoned DOE pilot smoothly ease along the hull of the alien ship, position his craft, then gently bring the rotation to a stop.

"This is something right out of the movies," Katy said.

"Yeah," Timothy said, "except this is real. Who or what is inside there?"

With the rotation stopped, Colonel Austin ordered the pilot to position the Omni-Star on the opposite side of the damaged vessel. Thirty minutes later, she was sitting a hundred feet off the port side of the wreck, looking into the huge rupture.

Jimmy ordered everyone to standby, then went to the communications room. He opened his wallet, pulled out a small card, and looked at the code for Seven at Spaceport Zeta. He made the connection and the call. Seven answered promptly.

"Seven, this is Colonel Austin, commander of Cosmos, now with the new ship, the Omni-Star."

"Yes, Colonel, I heard from Summar."

"Seven, on our way to the spaceport, we encountered a starship adrift in the outer region of the solar system's Oort Cloud, about a light-year from Earth. It's about a thousand feet long and two hundred or so, across. We are parked beside it right now."

"Colonel, do you see any markings on it?"

"Standby." Jimmy focused the communication lab's view screen on the ship, noticed some markings near the cente-rmost bulk of the ship's hull, and zoomed in on the strange insignia. "Yes, there's an emblem on the side. It's two large circles, one inside the other, then inside that there's a square with rounded corners. Again, inside that there's a sphere with a crown, like a king's crown, sitting on the sphere like a hat. Then, there's a rod on the bottom of the sphere that goes through the square, the two circles."

"Standby," Seven said, mimicking the colonel's word usage and tone. Moments later, his voice reappeared. "That's an Altairian ship. It was reported missing, presumed lost, two hundred and thirty years ago."

"Oh my God," Jimmy said. "It's been circling the solar system in our Oort Cloud for two hundred and thirty years?"

"Apparently. Have you gained entry?"

"No," Jimmy said electrically, "I wanted to call you first to see if you knew anything about it. We are about to do that. I'll let you know the results."

"I'll notify the Stationmaster Corps and the Altairians; they're members of the Alliance here. They will want to send a search and rescue ship to tow it home. Colonel, just for your information, the Altairians' ships have Electric Ion Propulsion and are equipped for suspended animation. You may find some of the crew asleep, maybe even all of them, if their animation system would handle that amount of time."

"Thank you, Seven. I'll let you know what we find."

Jimmy sat back. The picture was now getting serious. There was possibly a species of beings alive over there in that ship. He didn't know the Altairian language. However, Seven did. If anyone was alive and could successfully be awakened, he could call Seven and have him talk to them. *"Better still..."*, he thought. He keyed the intercom to the linguistics lab. "Two linguists, report to communications."

Momentarily, they arrived. He gave them Seven's code. "Call Seven and ask him to make this statement in the Altairian's language, and you record it for playback." **We are from Earth. We are on our way** *to Spaceport Zeta. We found your ship adrift. We will take you to the spaceport where you can make arrangements to get home*.

"Yes, sir," the linguists responded then turned to the equipment.

Jimmy went back to the bridge and viewed the alien ship again. The ancient disaster of the Titanic in 1912, on its maiden voyage, popped into his mind as he viewed the long tear in the side of the ancient starship. "Okay," Jimmy said, "two from the shuttle and one each from the DOEs, suit up and we'll go in as a team with hand thrusters. I'll join you. Hangar bay, fire up a guppy with full crew just in case and ferry me over so I can take a look inside that ship. Bruce, you have the bridge."

The navigator and safety officer from the shuttle joined Snyder and Abbott from the DOE's. When Colonel Austin arrived, suited and bearing a hand thruster, the five soon made their way into the breach in the side of the vessel, in the dim light of the distance sun. When inside, they turned on their helmet lights. A few objects, released from inertial force when the DOE stopped the ship's rotation, now floated about the vessel. One of them floated near Jimmy. He, recognizing the shape, reached out and grasped it. "Hey, look at this; it's a bow, as in bow and arrow. What's it doing on a starship?" He examined it closely, rubbing the wood with his thruster handle. "This looks like Bois D'arc wood. Gentlemen, this is from Earth. These aliens had been to Earth."

"I agree, Colonel," Snyder said, "look, attached to the wall there."

Jimmy looked at the three feet long wooden bar with its metal attachments in the middle and on each end. "What is it?"

"It's a single-tree." Snyder responded. "I saw one in a museum. It's a crossbar used to hook a horse to a wagon or a plow. The middle clamp is hooked to the load and chains are hooked to each end that go up to a collar worn by the horse or oxen. I'm originally from Kansas. The ancient Osage Indians lived there and used this type wood to make a lot of their tools and their bows."

"Ah," Jimmy said, "trinkets, souvenirs. These items would be about right from 230 years ago. They would have visited Earth around the year 1830. Okay, let's see if we can find the crew."

"A lot of them may have been lost out into space when this breach happened," Abbott offered. "It appears that the rupture was sudden and it's huge."

"We are forward of midship, let's make our way to the bridge."

Overhead was a mezzanine floor, metal grating, with hand rails on each side. The rails were about two and a half feet high on each side of the walkway. Gilbert Channing, Abbott's navigator, examined the walkway arrangement for a long moment. "Those handrails indicate that they are about four to five feet tall; pretty close to us."

"Yeah," Abbott responded, "how do we get up there: that probably leads to the bridge?"

"I see some stairs up ahead," Snyder said. "They also go through an opening in the floor and farther down into the ship."

They made their way to the ascending stairs and went up them. On the raised walkway they looked toward the bridge. Up ahead was a body. The one-piece suit was almost flat with the floor. The head was just a skeleton, which was wearing a respirator rig with a tank on his back.

"Apparently, he had time to get the oxygen mask on, however, the hard vacuum killed him," Jimmy said.

As they got closer, it became evident that the species of beings was different in appearance from human. The lower jaw of the skeleton protruded forward like the snout of a baboon. Otherwise, the general frame was similar to humans, with slightly longer arms.

They stepped over the body and continued on. Several more bodies were seen down on the floor below the walkway. Most were wearing respirators, to no avail. One of the crewmembers was lying on his side with one leg in a pressure suit; that being as far as he got before the pressure was gone and his body literally exploded from the inside. "This had to be a freak accident," Abbott said. They were caught completely by surprise."

Minutes later, they arrived at the bridge of the alien ship. There was only one body on the bridge. It was seated at the console. Its right hand was clutched over a larger button on the control panel.

"I'll bet that's the emergency beacon," Snyder said. "He managed to activate it before dying."

The crew was quiet for a moment. Jimmy turned and looked toward the stern of the vessel. "So far, there appears to be nobody alive on the ship. Seven said these people did use sleeping equipment on their starships. We'd better check all the compartments."

They went from compartment to compartment, looking inside every enclosure. Walking along the bottom half of the ship with the mezzanine floor overhead, they came to the hangar bay. There were two shuttles moored on board and one mooring station empty.

"Apparently," Jimmy said, "some of them managed to get into a shuttle and launch. It's about a light-year to Earth from here. I don't know if their shuttles had that much range. I guess it's possible they may have made it to Earth."

"Six trillion miles is a long journey for a small shuttle," Snyder added. "It's likely that their food and oxygen would run out before they could cross that much distance. These shuttles don't look like they would have lightspeed capability"

"We may never know," Jimmy said.

For the next hour, the five crewmembers checked one compartment after another, searching with hope to find a survivor. Then, from Abbot's navigator, the cry rang out; "In here, Captain; Colonel, it's a human!"

The rest of the team rushed in and gathered around the animation unit. It was a metal coffin-shaped box with a transparent window over the face of the figure inside.

DAN HOLT and MAX HOLT

Chapter 27

THE PASSENGER

Colonel Austin viewed the animation unit for several moments. "An Altairian starship, from 230 years ago, visit's Earth, then leaves. On their way out of the solar system, they suffer a freak accident, destroying their ship. There's only one survivor, a human from Earth. It looks like they abducted him. The fact that he's asleep, in the animation unit, is the reason he survived. Question; why is he the only one asleep?"

"Maybe he would know," Gil Channing offered.

"Maybe," Colonel Austin agreed. "Let's get him on board the Omni-Star and resume our transit to the spaceport. It will be better to wake him in a gravity environment. They probably put him to sleep while still on Earth. If I'm right about the year he is from; he's not going to know about weightlessness. He won't be able to understand why he doesn't weigh anything. I'll call Seven again and see if he knows anything about how their sleeping equipment works; the best way to revive him."

"Colonel," the pilot of the guppy parked outside the rupture said, "we have the equipment onboard to cut the unit loose to take it to the Omni-Star."

Jimmy walked around the animation unit, then noted the three-foot-long cylinder attached to the side of it. "Apparently, it's not attached to the ship or a gas supply. All it has is two clamps holding it on the floor. There's a cylinder attached to it, but it's part of the unit. Let's load it into the guppy and take it to the ship."

With the Omni-Star back in route to Spaceport Zeta and the animation unit in the clinic, the doctors, nurses, and several of the scientists stood around the human from, probably, the early 1800s. Jimmy singled out two of the doctors. "Come with me. Let's call Seven and see if he has any information about these Altairian animation units; how they engage them and, most importantly, how they awaken the person in a state of suspended animation."

The two doctors followed the Colonel to communications. They raised Seven. The Colonel outlined their situation. Seven, surprised when he was informed that there was a human aboard the Altairian vessel, asked the Colonel for a few minutes to review the library for information on the Altairian civilization. The Colonel complied.

Minutes later, Seven came back on line. *"Colonel, that human may have been abducted. The Altairians did take people from more primitive planets, up until about 200 years ago when the space council of Altair outlawed the practice. To answer your question, the Altairian animation unit puts the body in* **stasis**. *It's similar to the use of an anesthesia before medical procedures such as surgery, except it has an additional agent that suspends deterioration. To wake them, you simply turn off the valve to the supply tank and open* *the unit. The occupant will wake up in about thirty minutes."*

"Thank you, Seven. This rescue mission will make us a few days late arriving there. I'll call Little One and the Quantum Cloud and let them know."

DAN HOLT and MAX HOLT

Chapter 28

THE ABDUCTEE

With the ship underway, Colonel Austin asked Sharon and Katy from the bridge to come to the clinic and be visible to the awakening abductee. He felt that having two women present in the first group of people the awakened man from the eighteen-hundreds would see, might serve to dampen the shock for him. No one knew if he had actually seen his abductors with their vastly different features as humans. If he had, that image would be biting at his mind. If he had not, his sudden awakening in a strange place, among strange people, would be challenging, to say the least.

The team examined the animation unit thoroughly. It had four over center clamps holding a hinged lid tightly against soft surfaces, affecting a seal. Four of the team released the latches simultaneously and raised the lid. The human figure inside was dressed in his native garb; early western pants, shirt, and boots. He had long hair, down to the shoulders. He was about six feet tall, muscular, barrel chested, with rugged features. The doctors placed him at about thirty years old. Dr. Raymond Massey placed his stethoscope on his chest. He heard a very faint report about every six or eight seconds.

"He's handsome," Katy said.

Jimmy glanced at her, then back to the early American waiting for the induced stasis to wear off.

"Talk about getting your world turned upside down," Abbott said, "wait until he finds out where he is. Probably the greatest distance he's ever been from the earth is the height of his horse."

"And, the fastest he's ever traveled is the speed of the animal," Snyder added.

Minutes later, Dr. Massey placed his stethoscope on the sleeping form again and listened carefully. The report was now two seconds apart and much stronger. "He's coming around. He should be opening his eyes in a few minutes."

The waking abductee's breathing stabilized and became regular. He drew up one leg, then rubbed his face with both hands, then opened his eyes. When he saw the doctor above him, in a white coat, he positioned his hands and arms in a defensive posture.

"I'm a doctor," Raymond said quickly, "Dr. Massey. What's your name?"

There was silence for a long moment. "Brad, Brad Givens." The man quickly looked his body over, checking for an injury. Having not raised up yet, he had not noticed his surroundings. "Doc, what happened? How long have I been asleep?"

The doctor gestured toward Jimmy; the colonel stepped forward. "Brad," Dr. Massey said, "I'll let Colonel Austin answer those questions for you."

Brad sat up. "Ah, the Calvary; renegade Indians again?" His eyes, still blurry, went from Colonel Austin to the group of people standing around his unit. When he spotted Katy and Sharon, his focus locked on Sharon; he nodded in salutation. "Ma'am." Then looked her up and down, registering confusion at her one-piece jump suit.

Sharon responded. "Hi."

Katy nodded and smiled. Brad nodded again, then looked back to the colonel. "How long have I been asleep?"

Jimmy hesitated, thinking through his answer.

"Just give it to me straight, Colonel; three, four, days...a week?"

Jimmy decided to tell him what he must eventually know. "Two hundred and thirty years. This is going to be difficult to explain. Come with me; I want to show you something." Jimmy indicated the direction to the bridge.

Surprisingly, Brad stepped out of the unit easily. But when his vision cleared enough to see his surroundings, he froze in place, his heartbeat increasing rapidly. "Whoa! What is all this?! Where am I?! What are all these machines?!"

Jimmy grabbed his arm to steady him. "Brad, take it easy, just lean back against the chamber and breathe."

The pioneer's breathing slowed as he locked eyes with Jimmy. "Is this some sort of dream?" he muttered.

"No...no dream. It may be hard to believe at first, but you are on a space ship, uh...a flying machine. If you feel like walking, come with me and I will explain everything."

Brad balanced on his legs until he was steady. He looked around at the strange-looking people and nodded. "Okay, show me."

Jimmy headed out and the young man, over two centuries old, followed without hesitation. When they stepped through an arched doorway, the massive windshield was spread before them. The stars were blazing in their glory, sprinkling on a velvety black tapestry. Brad stared for moments, then his eyes found the colonel. "Are we really up in the sky?"

"Yes, all the way to where the stars are."

"I don't understand how I got here. Is this heaven; am I dead?"

Jimmy shook his head. "No, you're not. You're on a starship. What's the last thing you remember?"

"I was riding north of the river looking for a herd of wild horses. We heard they had been spotted close to the river. If you break them to ride, they bring good money."

"What river?"

"Red River; Oklahoma Territory."

Colonel Austin, hoping the question and answer exchange would help Brad come to grips with what has happened, fielded the next question. "What day was that?"

Jimmy's revelation of how long he had been asleep hadn't yet registered in Brad's mind. "I don't know how long I've been asleep. It must have been at least a few days ago. It was June 2nd."

"What year?"

"What year?!" Brad said in an astounded tone. "This year—1831."

Jimmy locked eyes with Brad Givens. "Brad, today is August 12; the year is 2061. You have been in that sleeping chamber for two hundred and thirty years."

Brad stared at Colonel Austin for a long moment, then turned back to the spread of stars outside the windshield, and then looked at the floor.

Jimmy could tell he was struggling to process this new reality. "Tell me the last thing you remember before you woke up here."

Brad looked at Jimmy again. "I was riding along the river, among the bushes, shrubs, with trees here and there, looking around for evidence of the horses, their tracks, droppings, and all. It was a hot day; the sun was really hot. Suddenly, it got a lot brighter. I stopped and looked up. It blinded me, like the brightest sun I had ever seen. The next thing I saw was that doctor wearing that white coat. For a minute, I thought I was dead."

"This is really hard for me to explain to you. Just trust me for now. You were abducted by people that came down from the sky."

"Abducted? What does abducted mean?"

"Kidnapped, knocked out and taken while you were unconscious. They put you in this box and put you to sleep like doctors do when they operate on you. Then, when flying away from Earth, their luck went bad and they wrecked their ship. We found it. They were all dead. However, you were lucky; we found you still okay, sleeping in that thing in the clinic."

"Wait a minute, Colonel, you mean that I am 230 years into the future from where I was when I was looking for them horses?"

"Yes."

Brad Givens was quiet for some time. His gaze went back to the windshield and the thousands of stars outside. In his field of view was the crew of three still at the helm of the ship. He gestured toward them. "They drivin this thing?"

Colonel Austin nodded.

"Where we goin?"

"To Spaceport Zeta. It's a way-station in space. Later, we'll be going back to Earth."

Colonel Austin gestured toward the seats aligned along the windshield on either side of the bridge crew seating. Brad walked over, with the colonel, and sat down, viewing the stars and occasionally looking around the main deck of the starship. He turned toward Jimmy. "What do I do now?"

"Well, we are in route to Spaceport Zeta. It's a stopover, like a boarding house. It's a ball, a sphere, a hundred miles in diameter; it's a big place. It was built in space as a place to stop over and rest, resupply, or simply visit and enjoy. We'll show you around. We are going there to do some research in their library. We need some information that we think may be there.

From there, we may visit another planet, then we'll return to Earth. When we do, we'll research your family history. Did you have any children?"

"Two; a boy, Henry, 12, and a girl, Sarah 8. Aw, man, they think I took off and abandoned them, don't they. And, Lidia; she's going to be wondering where I am."

"Brad, they are all dead and gone. About two hundred years ago."

It was clear on Brad's face that he was struggling to comprehend. Jimmy continued. "We'll research your family tree and see if we can find your great, great, great grandchildren. If we find some of them, when we get back to Earth, we'll take you to visit them. They will look up to you. They will want to know everything about hunting wild horses."

Jimmy contacted the ship's library and assigned two of the historians to Brad, to take him to the aft lounge for a meal, and then see that he was assigned quarters and issued fresh clothing. Next, they were to prepare him for a few hours of weightlessness when the ship went through the procedures of approaching the spaceport, entering, and docking; admittedly, no easy task.

Further, they were to introduce Brad to the reality of the giants, now a part of man's world. He would be introduced to the school teacher on board. It was an opportunity for Brad to spend the next few months and be brought up to date and for the new teacher to get some practice. It would be a difficult adjustment.

However, the eighteenth-century man seemed resilient. Jimmy also suggested that the historians contact NASA back on Earth and, through them, the Historical Society of Houston and petition them to do a thorough search through the ancestral archives on Brad Givens and report the findings to the Omni-Star.

James Rawlins and Wendell Bain, historians, sitting with Brad in the aft lounge, ordered themselves an evening meal of soup with a fruit plate. Brad, still learning, nodded for the same. Then he looked at the waiter. "If you have any, I sure would like to have a fresh tomato. Uh...and a salt shaker." The waiter smiled and left to place their orders.

James and Wendell decided to address weightlessness first. Wendell turned to Brad. "Brad, did you go to school when you younger?"

"Yes," Brad responded, "there was a schoolhouse at the edge of Wichita where we lived when my father was working cattle on the Chisholm Trail. I went to it for three years."

"Good. Did you learn about the solar system and the planets, and about gravity?"

Brad frowned. "No, I don't remember nothing about that. I learned to read and write pretty good. Also, we did arithmetic and spelling. And, we learned a little about the oceans, sailing ships and foreign countries; stuff like that, but I don't remember much of it."

"I want to talk to you about weightlessness. I want to prepare you for what's coming when we approach the space station ahead. It's still months away, but when we arrive you are going to be weightless for a number of hours on the final approach and entry to the station."

"What does that mean, exactly? How is it possible to weigh nothing?" Brad said.

"It has to do with gravity, like I was talking about earlier. The size of the earth, about 8,000 miles across, determines how much you weigh. Gravity is like a magnet or a load stone. You know a load stone will pick up nails or a horseshoe."

"Yeah."

"Well, gravity attracts everything, not just iron, everything, including us. When we get to the space station and start slowing down, we'll be away from all the planets like Earth and we will weigh nothing—zero weight. You will feel like you are falling all the time. Do you think you can handle that?"

"I think so. When I was seventeen or eighteen, me and two other guys jumped off a cliff, about thirty feet high, into the river. It made my stomach queasy on the way down."

"That's what I wanted you to understand. When we arrive, we are all going to be weightless for, possibly, several hours."

"I'll be okay."

"If, for some reason, it becomes too serious for you to handle, we have the equipment to put you to sleep, until we are in the station and gravity is back."

"I've had enough sleep for a while," Brad said and grinned.

James and Wendell looked at each other, their eyes relaying a message, the witnessing of the beginnings of true adjustment to a world completely new.

Chapter 29

SPACEPORT ARRIVAL

The Omni-Star began slowing. Sheldon Darcy, fresh from Cosmos, now with well over a year's experience piloting the Omni-Star, saw the space station sphere, growing in size. Radio contact with Zeta Control had verified their clearance to land at the way-station, in the same berth as Cosmos had used. Having not been to Spaceport Zeta before, he looked over at the copilot and spoke quietly. "Where's the door."

Timothy smiled. "It's around to the right from here. It's on the Zannian side of Zeta.

"Mooring number 22," Colonel Austin interjected. Inside, take a left, it's about a mile or so to parking. Very slowly, Mr. Darcy; no fender benders."

"Sheldon smiled. "Yes, sir."

The Omni-Star drifted into the gas barrier at Zeta's entrance. Sheldon was holding his breath. He noticed, then glanced around, and took a breath. He felt his weight returning. He negotiated a left turn and began traversing the final mile or so to the mooring that was waiting for the ship from Earth. Zeta had added lighted mooring signs since their last visit. Sheldon noticed right away the sign, flashing the name, OMNI-STAR.

"Look, Colonel," Timothy said, spotting the two other recent arrivals settled into their moorings, "it's Little One and the Quantum Cloud. Mentar and Summar are both already here. We park between them. This will make it easy to transfer the cargo for Zannia. I'll get that coordinated after the crew's first shore leave."

"Sounds good. I'll check with Mentar about moving the passengers to Little One."

Katy spoke up. "What about Brad?"

The colonel thought. "Well, for now he stays with us, until we return to Earth. I'm sure NASA is already checking his family tree. I hope they can locate some of his family descendants. Whatever happens, it will take him a long time to adjust to the new world."

Sheldon maneuvered the ship into the mooring space and set it down. He noticed a light come on at the base of the wall in front of the ship. Somewhere in the heart of Spaceport Zeta, accounting equipment recorded the arrival of another starship, probably with its tonnage, origin, and purpose.

Colonel Austin ordered the ship at Station-Keeping, with a minimum number of rotor pods remaining online. "All personnel may exercise shore leave except for the skeleton crews, which will rotate on and off-duty as per regulations. While we are here, which could be for some time, let's maintain the daily cycle of meals and sleeping periods on Earth schedule. There's going to be a lot of study and investigation, as well as touring and entertainment offerings. We don't want to lose anybody. Promptly report any problems or mishaps, should any occur. Enjoy your visit to Spaceport Zeta."

The first officer set up the skeleton crews and their replacement arrangements, then released all others to shore leave. A mass exit of the ship's personnel did not happen immediately. Many of the new spacefarers were taking their time to adjust from the ordeal of several hours of weightlessness, waiting for the touch of nausea to subside.

The adjustment was relatively quick and the curious began to disembark. Jimmy, Bruce, and the bridge crew, invited James, Wendell, Brad, and Venataar to experience this huge metal *island* hanging in deep space. The twelve from Earth exited the ship.

At the bottom of the ramp, they looked toward Little One and saw **Zolaadine Man**, the large damaged robot Mentar had brought from Zannia. It had just been unloaded from the ship and was laying on its side on a shipping pallet that had been loaded onto a cargo trailer. Jimmy walked over and spoke to an android that was securing it with straps.

Assuming it could speak English, he asked, "Where are you taking it?"

"Mentar, a Zannian, requested analysis of this ancient machine. We are taking it to the Deep Space Research Group, in the basement of the Library. They will do a thorough analysis relative to its level of technology. It may give a clue where to start looking for its creators. Also, they will attempt to repair it."

Jimmy nodded. "Thanks. I'll check with Mentar later for the results."

As he turned to go, the android asked, *"Aren't you the Captain of the Omni-Star?"*

Jimmy stopped. "Yes, we just landed."

"Sir, after we deliver this robot, we have instructions to offload a statue from your ship and place it in the Museum. Will we have access to your cargo hold?"

"Yes, we brought a Moai statue from Earth to be displayed here at Zeta. It is a representation of the giant humanoids you have seen here recently. A small crew will be on duty continuously during our stay, so you'll have access anytime. Please handle the Moai carefully."

"Will do, sir, we want everyone to see that amazing artifact."

As the crew headed into the spaceport, the android, Seven, having been alerted, met them when they stepped through the large arched doorway.

"Hello, Seven," Colonel Austin said. "This is James Rawlins and Wendell Bain, historians from Earth, and this is Brad Givens, the abductee from the nineteenth century, the one we called you about; and, of course, you know my bridge crew." He turned to his new giant friend. "This is Venataar, one of Mentar's fellow survivors from Earth's moon. He and six others were recently found in a lab that was buried in the ancient disaster. He is a botanical researcher."

Seven extended his hand over his head and stretched it up to meet the giant's grip. *"Welcome to*

Zeta, Venataar. Mentar mentioned that you were coming. He is anxious to greet you."

Venataar smiled. "I am looking forward to seeing him and, soon, my original home planet, although I've never actually been there. While I'm here I would request to visit your farms and hydroponic spaces."

"Of course, I can arrange that."

Seven nodded toward James, Wendell, and the crew, then turned to Brad. *"I would like to talk to you about the time-period in which you were living on Earth."*

Brad had been pushed to the edge of understanding when he met Venataar on the ship. He was still staggered by the giant's size and deep voice. Now, here was another kind of *being* altogether. Locking eyes with Seven he said spontaneously, "You are a machine!"

"Yes," Seven responded, *"I'm an android. In human terms, I could be considered as a mechanical man.*

"But you're talking."

Seven's pause was just over two milliseconds. His data banks projected the best response, based on the current information he had on a Brad Givens. *"Yes. The humanoids that built me taught me how to talk and do things. I'm supposed to assist you while you are here."*

As Seven finished his sentence, two Athenians flew by, each carrying a briefcase. Brad stepped back and caught his breath; he was speechless. Seven put his android hand on Brad's arm. *"Just relax, Mr. Givens, you still have a lot to catch up on."*

Brad nodded, then smiled nervously at Jimmy and the rest of the party. Seven stepped over and activated one of the transports and moved it into position for the twelve 'tourists' to board.

"Seven," Jimmy said, "where are Mentar, Kronos, and Summar?"

"They are at Spirit's and Song. They are waiting for you. They requested to be informed upon your arrival. They were informed that your rescue of Mr. Givens delayed you."

"Okay, take us there."

Seven promptly engaged the route to the facility. Jimmy turned to Brad. "Brad, you are about to meet two other giants. One is 12 feet tall, the other is a full 40 feet tall, like Venataar. I want you to prepare yourself. They are friends of mine. The bigger one, Mentar, is one of the giants that James and Wendell told you about. On his planet, everybody is about 40 feet tall except about 350 Earth people that now live there."

Brad was trying to take it all in. "Like I told them, while I was going to school, after I learned to read pretty good, my teacher had a copy of Gulliver's Travels and she let me read it. It was about giants and little people. My teacher said it was fiction, not true, but was written as a fun story. I didn't know there was real giants"

"We didn't either until the end of the twentieth century. I bought a copy of that book," Jimmy said, "and gave it to Mentar to read; he's the other 40-foot-tall giant you are about to meet."

"The giants in the book were 72 feet tall."

"Yeah, I know. I thought Mentar might find that interesting. By the way, Mentar's the one that first named us *Little Ones*."

Brad was quiet for a few moments as the space station wonders passed by the transport. "Colonel, I keep looking around, trying to accept all of this. I keep wondering if I'm going to wake up under a tree by the river, lying on my saddle blanket, and all this is a dream."

"I'm afraid not. This has got to be very awkward for you, but you are here, and you are alive, and this is your new reality. It should help if we find some of your family when we get back home."

Seven brought the transport to a stop in the parking area of the entertainment facility. He set the machine down in place, disembarked and turned to his charges. "Follow me."

Sharon slid over close to Brad. "Get ready to see some very different …uh, people here."

"Yeah, the colonel told me there were going to be some giants in here."

"There's also going to be other people…uh, beings close to our size but different appearance; some will be smaller."

Seven led the way into the club and lounge with his charges following in single file. He turned left inside the door and headed for the far wall. In the dim light, they were within fifty feet when the crew spotted the special table and chair arrangement. Mentar, Summar, and Kronos raised their hands and arms in salutation. Jimmy responded. The hundred or so patrons watched in amusement.

When Jimmy and company waved, smiling, then went up the few steps to their level and seated themselves; the crowd cheered for a moment, then gradually, few by few, went back to their own affairs. They had had several days to get used to the novelty of seeing the largest known humanoid personally and, finally, discovering that the giants' best friends topped off at about their kneecaps.

Venataar stepped ahead of the others. He yelled out in moon: "Mentar! It's so good to see you! I long to see Zannia and what you have accomplished there."

Mentar and Kronos gave him the traditional Zannian greeting, and then Mentar added a hug. Venataar released and then said, "I see you learned much from the *little ones*."

Mentar nodded, "Yes, and we are still learning. I have much to tell you about our home planet. We will have time to discuss it on the way, in a few days.

Mentar then greeted Jimmy and his crew.

"How did you get this table?" Jimmy asked.

Mentar nodded toward Seven. "The android ordered it over the radio. Four other androids delivered it about half an hour later. That must be some workshop they've got here."

"How long have you been here?"

"Six days."

"Sorry about being so late. We had to make a stop and pick up this guy," Colonel Austin said, indicating Brad.

"Seven told us. Lucky for him that you were passing by his way." Mentar looked around. "Where is the school teacher you brought for the colony?"

"Yes, Lilah Owenby...she is Jack and Brenda's granddaughter."

Mentar smiled. Yes, I know. You should see the excitement in those grandparents. They have been preparing for her like a bird prepares a nest."

"I'm sure. As soon as you arrived, she requested to go straight to the Zeta school that educates the children of the permanent Zeta staff. You will meet her tomorrow. She will need to transfer her belongings to your ship."

As Brad looked up at Mentar, the giant nodded. Brad nodded back then looked at the colonel, then his eyes went to Sharon. "He's huge, too."

Sharon laughed. "Yeah, we found him on the moon, about sixty years before we found Venataar."

"Yeah, that's what James and Wendell told me. These giants were on the moon, in a tunnel, for thousands of years."

An android showed up at the table with twelve additional drinks, based on Seven's memory banks. Brad eyed the tiny column of smoke spiraling up from the amber liquid. He looked at Sharon with question and caution on his countenance. She smiled, then picked up her glass and took a sip. "It's harmless, it's a special touch they add for appearance."

Brad picked it up and took a sip, then nodded. "It's good."

A pure refrain of a stringed instrument flowed through the club. All eyes went to the stage. Brad's followed. "My God, that's the biggest guitar I've ever seen."

"That's Javienne," Sharon said. "We know him; he was found on the moon, too…he's really good."

Javienne began singing the well-known ballad in the Moon language. The club slowly became quiet. The haunting sounds seem to mesmerize. The words, understood only by Mentar, Kronos, and Seven, captured the audience, none the less. Spirits and Song was completely quiet until the last refrain slowly faded. Javienne, in the stillness, nodded to the audience, then rejoined his colleagues at the table. Gradually, the noises of diverse life returned.

"Now, you are going to be known around the galaxy," Jimmy said. "I wonder how many here are now homesick."

Javienne smiled and took a sip of his drink.

Kronos and Venataar excused themselves. Kronos had agreed to go help the new arrival move his belongings from the Omni-Star over to Little One for the pending trip to Zannia…and *home,*

Jimmy looked at Mentar. "We have requested wormhole training and have a tentative schedule to enter the Vortex in three days. When are you returning to Zannia?"

"We are flexible on departure time. We still have a lot to explore here at Zeta and much to learn about…everything. I will wait until you finish your training and you are ready to depart on your mission of discovery. Then, we will say our goodbyes and our ships will depart for Zannia."

"Ships? You only have Little One, right?"

"Yes, but Zeta is sending a cargo ship with us. They will return to Zeta with a load of Zolaadine I sold them yesterday."

Jimmy's whole crew had a look of surprise.

Mentar continued. "Turns out, many planets' ships can't enter the wormhole because they don't have qualifying outer shells on the hulls to withstand the stresses in the tunnel. Zeta decided to stock Zolaadine and market the necessary coatings to new member planets. We will get a free coating for Little One. I believe you Earthlings have an old saying: *Make a buck anyway you can.*"

A broad smile covered Jimmy's face. "My, my…Mentar, I do believe you are the biggest *human* I ever met."

Everyone laughed.

As Jimmy and crew were congratulating Mentar on his entrepreneur ability, Katy's assistant came into the room carrying a printed message in her hand. She handed it to Katy, who read it, and then turned to the colonel, searching for the words to say.

Jimmy sat his drink down. "Katy, what is it?"

"NASA has completed their research of Brad's family tree. They were able to find a great, great, great granddaughter and her son. They are both alive and well."

Brad blurted out: "Hot dog! Now I'll have a family to share my life with!"

"Congratulations, Brad, I'm happy for you. As soon as we get back to Earth, we will give you a free ride to wherever they are."

Katy spoke up. "Colonel, they are on Zannia with the colonists."

"What?"

Katy smiled, then held up the NASA message and read: *"Rebecca Givens Weston, daughter of David and Leona Givens, and her son Jeremy Weston, departed as part of the Zannian colony fifteen years ago."*

After a few moments, Jimmy found his voice. "Jeremy Weston...the tomato kid?"

"Yes, sir, that's the one."

Brad looked at Jimmy. "What do you mean, tomato kid?"

Jimmy explained the tomato incident in the engine room of Discovery, when Jeremy was eight years old.

Brad smiled. "Well, he comes by it natural...I love tomatoes. And, if it is all the same to you, Colonel, I'd like to try my hand on that Zannia planet...I have family there."

"I'm glad," Jimmy said, then looked up at Mentar.

He nodded, "I have plenty of room on Little One."

After a moment of quiet, Brad interjected, "How did a group of giants name their starship Little One?"

"It's a long story," Jimmy said, "your granddaughter can tell you all about it."

DAN HOLT and MAX HOLT

Chapter 30

THE SUPERMARKET

Colonel Austin and several members of the older caucus of scientists were enjoying their evening meal, Earth-time. Jimmy described many of the things seen during the previous visit on Zeta. He recommended that the scientists take a couple of days and tour the facility for the experience and to have the knowledge of what the spaceport offered. The scientists agreed, although they were anxious to get into the data banks of the extensive library. They wanted to begin the vigilant search for the location of the mysterious Moai and what it might reveal.

Howard Wiggins, 'Starman,' a *heavy* among the scientists aboard, suggested that they take the advice and do a thorough tour of Zeta. His insistence was: they should know about all that's here; there may be important information or a service that would be very beneficial to their cause.

The large body of scientists, divided up into groups of forty, began the vigil of getting to know Spaceport Zeta. Jimmy recommended they start with the farms, the museum, and the wormhole vortex. That magic word, *wormhole,* sparked instant interest. They knew it was real. But, if it was actually workable for the Omni-Star; if it was a safe mode of star travel, it opened up fantastic possibilities. Lords of the galaxy? No, ...students of the galaxy.

The Supermarket

Colonel Austin, his bridge crew, Mentar, Kronos, and Javienne finished their soup entries at Aisle Side Lounge and were viewing the menu for a fruit entre to top off their meal. An android approached. *"Colonel, Mentar, we have set aside space for your starship's offerings in the supermarket."*

"Supermarket?"

"Yes. Zeta installed a cuisine interactive eatery for use of visiting starships. You now have an assigned area where you may exhibit the foods produced on your starship for the citizens of different worlds to sample and enjoy anytime you are in port. Of course, you and your ships company may indulge as well. It's four floors down at the center of the station. Transports will assist you with moving you stocks to the market."

Jimmy nodded. "I'll notify Omni-Star's farms and hydroponics. This I've got to see, and sample."

Summar spoke up. 'We restocked our area just after we arrived. You must try some of our vegetables, some of which are grown in very warm soil. The originals on our planet are produced near the base of an active volcano."

"I'll do that," Jimmy responded, then turned to Mentar. "That's a good idea. When we're docked, we go into surplus anyway."

"Yes, it is," agreed Mentar.

Jimmy notified the Omni-Star and gave the android the nod. Upon finishing his fruit, he and his colleagues arose and headed for the supermarket for a tour. In transit, Jimmy looked up at Mentar. "This is good timing. They say: never go shopping when you are hungry."

"Why not?" Mentar asked.

"Because you will over-buy and spend too much money."

Mentar frowned, then: "Oh, yes. Earth and it's money system."

"Yeah."

"I have some experience with that. I made a good deal there almost sixty years ago," Mentar said and smiled coyly.

"Yeah, I read about that. Did you know that a total was estimated on the bounty you presented to Earth from your original abandoned star ship? Once we learned how to salvage it from Saturn's orbit, it paid for Little One several times over?"

"So, it was a good deal for Earth, too."

"Yes, yes it was."

Mentar was quiet for a few moments as the miles rolled by, then he addressed Jimmy again. "Colonel, I would like to open a line of credit with Earth."

Jimmy paused, then looked up at Mentar. "Are you serious?"

"Yes, for 500 rotor pods and support parts for the same. We will need them for our new starship, under construction, and those to follow. Parliament on

Zannia has been debating this for some time. Earth's magnets are superior; the neodymium-rare-earth magnets. They put the pods at full power."

"I read what Colonel Andrews, commander Discovery, asked you on that deal; what method of payment?"

"How about a starship full of pure Zolaadine?"

"Mentar, you know how to bargain. Let's put the commerce people together and let them work it out. Interstellar trade; this is a first for Earth."

"And Zannia," Mentar endorsed.

The android chauffer stopped the transport in front of the entrance to the supermarket. The party disembarked and entered the well-lighted space. The entire room was walled with mirrors. The effect was awesome. It was cool inside the facility and it was equipped with water sprinkling systems above the fruits and vegetables. There were spaces completely empty of produce, others with only a few items left, and still others very prolific with fresh items. The crew walked down the aisles looking at the different sizes and colors of, apparently, the same or sister species of foods.

"This is amazing, Colonel," Melvin said, indicating a ten-foot by ten-foot bin with a couple dozen red sphere-shaped food items. "These are tomatoes, the size of basketballs."

"Apparently," Kronos interjected, "there are other planets with Zannian-like soil, rich with nutrients."

"I'd like to know where the planet is that these came from," Mentar said.

"And, perhaps, someday, go and visit them," Javienne added. "They may be our size."

"That would be something," Jimmy commented, then looked across the expanse of the supermarket. "Wait until our scientists see this. Another field of study. Soon, the universities of Earth will be offering off-world electives to the world of academia."

Brad picked up one of the tomatoes. "Now, that's a tomato!"

"We grow them like that on Zannia," Mentar offered.

"Good, good," Brad responded. "Me and my great-grandson can pick up a couple of salt shakers and take an afternoon walk to the tomato fields." Bran looked at Mentar, grinning.

"You are an interesting man, Mr. Givens. You'll make a good Zannian."

DAN HOLT and MAX HOLT

Chapter 31

THE STUDY

The graduate students aboard Omni-Star petitioned the androids to transport them to the library. They wanted a list of the planets that were now members of the alliance here at Spaceport Zeta. They would visit each research station and check the location and magnitude of the star they were orbiting, as well as any other significant signatures or identifiers of the planet's home star. They were attempting to develop a clear signature of a star that was known to be supporting life. Perhaps there were clear and definite signs that could identify more stars that are, more than likely, supporters of sentient life.

The seasoned scientists lauded the efforts of the young researchers. They were focused on a field of research that would further the science of astronomy. They were clearly developing one more tool to aid in getting to know the Universe.

The students, arriving at the library entrance, organized themselves in parties of two to enter and research the host star of each planet represented at the Spaceport. The vigil began.

Amil Lajadha, India, and Connie Singleton, America, entered the enclosure for the planet, Lindia, a planet that was located some twelve light-years from

Zeta. Amil had his tablet-like device to record the sought-after stats on the planet. When they entered the study area, there was a Lindian female sitting at one of the tables studying something on the screen of one of the monitors built into the table. She was just over six feet tall and had a blueish skin tone. Her eyes were about twice the diameter as those of a human.

Amil studied her face and eyes for a long moment. She noticed his scrutiny and glanced in his direction, then back to her monitor. Amil introduced himself. She shook her head, holding his eyes.

"She doesn't understand me," Amil muttered. He held up one finger then hurried to the entrance and petitioned the android to accompany him back into the study area. The machine did so. He spoke to the lady again. The android interpreted. *"My name is Amil. I am from Earth. I would like to ask you some questions about your planet."*

Upon the android's answer, her eyes went from his face to Amil's with a look of question. "I am Meta," she said, getting to her feet.

Amil, looking up into her eyes, saw a depth that was challenging. He cleared his throat. "I noticed that you have exceptional eyesight. How far is your planet from its star?"

She answered, then glanced at the android. He turned to Amil. *"In Earth measure, It's one hundred forty-eight million miles or 13.26 light minutes."*

The female visitor from Lindia spoke again. Amil looked at the android. *"She wants to know why you ask."*

Amil looked at her and smiled. "Two reasons. One, I'm doing a study to see if there's a subtle auroral signature that I could look for that would tell me the probability of a planet being inhabited, and two, upon discovering your exceptional eyesight, I wondered if it was an evolutionary product of a dimmer star."

Upon the android's answer, Meta reached and took Amil by the hand and led him across the study area to a row of cabinets. The android followed. She pulled one of the drawers open. It was filled with small data-chips. "All of Lindia's statistics are here," she said, releasing his hand.

"Thank you," Amil said.

She smiled, then turned and went back to her studies.

The fifty graduate students, at two per study station, were busily investigating and recording the information on the fifty-one stars that were represented here. Earth was already thoroughly studied, and now, even from afar. These fifty-one were special. They all supported a planet harboring life, intelligent life, and they each had different statistics. The challenge of these new astronomers recently unleased on the world, was to find the common thread, the signature that would indicate that life is present in a system.

DAN HOLT and MAX HOLT

Chapter 32

THE SCIENTISTS

Following the research in the Library, the 120 scientists from planet Earth came back together for a meeting. Much had been studied in route to the spaceport. To many of the scientists' delight, they were able to verify many conclusions reached through study of the heavens from the surface of Earth, amid the handicaps of the atmosphere, weather, and, of course, the distances. Other assumed facts had been disproved and would have to be addressed again.

There was also the incident of the wrecked alien ship, a stark reminder of the hazardous business of space travel. Plus, to the delight of the ship's company, there was the miraculous rescue of a citizen of earth from an earlier time and involving a different civilization with different science. An incident that introduced them to a variation on the higher technology that had been discovered when they found the giants on Earth's moon—suspended animation. The scientists now had aboard the animation unit for study.

But now, parked at Spaceport Zeta, the suppository of an immense amount of information pertaining to the galaxy and fifty-two of her member planets, the task lay before them. The quest, the reason for the creation of the Omni-Star. The senior astronomers felt sure that here, in this spaceport, more than likely, was the information that would lead them to some answers. Answers that all on Earth were waiting for.

There was no key search word, no heading, that would lead directly to the information. Instead, it would have to be a plodding, record-by-record search, looking for mention of an item on some planet that could possibly be a Moai. They wanted to get all their researchers organized into search teams and set criteria to prevent passing over it without recognizing that they had found the prize.

The meeting, aboard the Omni-Star, produced ten teams of six each, chosen by lottery. The scientists wanted the best chance of success, not necessarily camaraderie. They entered Zeta's extensive library again and began their search with renewed purpose.

They spread themselves into ten of the planets, starting with the closest and then moving outward, exempting, of course, Earth and Zannia. A team in each study area; each with an interpreting machine. The teams quickly found that it was a daunting task. They weren't there ten minutes until one entered the search word, Moai. Of course, it yielded nothing as the name for the coveted statue was assigned to it by Earth. Its true name was yet to be known.

There were multiple categories or trails in the planetary records to follow that could lead to possibilities. Monuments. Statues. Memorials. Sculpting. Art. Honorariums. And the list went on. They decided to start with the obvious—Statues.

The remaining sixty scientists would dedicate themselves to understanding wormhole travel. They petitioned the Stationmaster Corps for a complete seminar on the phenomenon up to and including actual wormhole travel under the guidance of the androids.

And so, the vigil for a destination and the capability to get there, was on.

DAN HOLT and MAX HOLT

Chapter 33

The Training

The next morning, Jimmy and his bridge crew reported to Zeta Engineering, with Seven leading the way. They were scheduled for two days of intense procedural training necessary for them to safely negotiate wormhole travel. They would get the advantage of centuries of experience and trial-and-error by the crews of other ships that had safely negotiated the *time tunnels* across the galaxy.

The group of scientists were given access to all the records compiled on wormholes and began pouring over the bulbous cache of information. They soon discovered that the Zannian scientists had actually created a partial wormhole when they designed the Waddell Cone. Those massive generators created a weak dark energy field! It was why the starships now traveled much faster with the same power expenditure. However, the field was not the pure thing; nothing like the dark energy that a galaxy could produce.

The first order of business was a thorough examination of the structural integrity of the Omni-Star. The engineers determined that the titanium shell on the outside of the hull was sufficient to withstand the stresses of wormhole transit speeds.

The first phase of training was Wormhole Analysis. They learned that wormholes were not stationary; they swayed and twisted as they meandered through space. As could best be determined, the fabric of space inside the wormhole was a combination of Dark Matter and Dark Energy. The Dark Matter made up the **walls** of the tunnel and the Dark Energy, the *river* flowing through it.

Wormholes varied in diameter, from ten miles to as much as 100 miles. When a starship, or anything for that matter, entered the wormhole Vortex it automatically assumed a negative field and the positive field of the flowing river of Dark Energy pulled it along at fantastic velocities. Since all ships that were introduced to the wormhole system were automatically negatively charged, there was no danger of two ships, traveling in different directions, colliding with each other. Like-fields repel; a natural law guaranteeing a clear path through the wormhole. Upon reaching a Vortex, a place where all fields are neutral, or equalized, the ships would come to a stop. At that point, the ship could exit the system or choose to continue on in whatever tunnels connect to that Vortex.

"What about inertial forces with the ship jumping to such exaggerated speeds upon entering the wormhole?" Sharon, ship's safety officer, inquired.

"They are canceled. The Dark Energy attracts everything, just like gravity, therefore, you feel none of the inertial forces involved. It fact, it's believed that Dark Energy is a by-product of gravity; a sister force, as it were. Now," Seven continued, *"Let's take an*

actual flight through the wormhole in your ship. In your case, I recommend a trip to the Vortex in your solar system and then a return since your system is relatively close."

"How long with it take to get there and back?" Melvin asked.

"The average wormhole speed is about a day per light-year's distance. The journey will be about seven and a half days, flight time."

"Oh my God," Bruce said. "That's amazing!"

"Remember though," Seven emphasized, *"when you exit the Vortex, you still have to transit from the Vortex to your destination at normal velocities. You may still have a month's travel time, Vortex to destination. The wormhole system puts you in the vicinity of your destination, which really helps, especially on the longer voyages."*

DAN HOLT and MAX HOLT

Chapter 34

THE TUNNEL

Colonel Austin recalled all the compliment of the Omni-Star back aboard for a temporary hiatus to experience wormhole travel. It would be an android-chaperoned, by Seven and four other android colleagues, maiden voyage to the Earth's solar system Vortex.

Electricity was in the air as the starship approached the Vortex near Spaceport Zeta. All the compliment of the ship was seated and buckled in for the initial entrance into the system. The posturing was recommended by Seven as a prudent caution for the initial experience. It was new to all, except the androids, and no one wanted a freak accident under the influence of adrenaline.

"Colonel,' Seven said, *"We recommend that when you enter a Vortex and the influence begins pulling your ship forward, you throttle back to zero with your engines. When you reach the next Vortex and the influence releases you, your ship will come to a stop and allow you decision time on whether to continue in the system or to exit the Vortex. If you leave your power engaged, your ship will continue through the Vortex at its set speed and enter the next wormhole in the direction it's facing."*

"Understood."

"We have mapped this wormhole system and will provide you with a downloaded computer copy. That will help you pick the closest Vortex to you intended destination."

Sheldon Darcy steered the Omni-Star into the throat of the Vortex. He, the first officer, and the colonel, commanding the starship were comfortable with a seasoned and well-known android standing on the bridge. The android's assistants were placed in the engine room, communications, maintenance, and the science lab. All expressed the demeanor of a routine day; a comforting posture for the surrounding crew of the starship.

The ship nudged ahead at its normal power setting. Seven then instructed the bridge crew: *"Zero power."*

Sheldon immediately disengaged the rotor pods. The engine room grew quiet.

Chief Matthew Dolan looked across his sea of rotor pods, then at the android. The starship was accelerating, and his rotor pods were all quiet except the basic power-generating cluster, running in a quieted mode. However, they all stood running at zero thrust, but ready to do their job.

All eyes were on the windshield for a look at the phenomenon of a wormhole highway, leading through raw space. They watched the cone of the Vortex pass behind the ship while it constantly gained speed. The tunnel ahead looked like a huge soda straw that had been used in a glass of milk. It sped by faster and faster. The ship felt completely still and smooth. Occasionally a nudge could be felt as the wormhole meandered gently side to side. The stars would show that the ship was rotating a few degrees from time to time, then slowly returning to the original orientation.

Soon, Seven addressed the colonel. *"You may continue your normal routine. The ship is up to speed. We will arrive at the Vortex in about three and a half days."*

The ship's company spent the first few hours favoring the windshield and the portholes, mesmerized at the speed at which the ship was traveling. The scientists, out of curiosity, attempted to lock a telescope on a distant star system. The computers would not accept the command. They were moving through space much faster than the light coming from the target. Tracking, even under the speeds of the Waddell Cone, was close to the maximum capability of the system.

Early afternoon of day four, the Omni-Star exited the Vortex, tucked into the edge of the Kuiper Belt. Ahead was the fiery heart of the solar system. It was between two and a half and three months away under standard starship transit speed. Zeta was three and a half days away, via the wormhole. Many had difficulty wrapping their minds around that fact. If one was going to traverse star to star, the wormhole was the best answer. Otherwise, the galaxy, relative to man and many other sentient beings, would be lots of wasted space, never to be visited. Perhaps someone awesome knew that, and constructed an answer for those bold enough to climb the tree of knowledge, high enough to find it.

Chapter 35

THE DESTINATION

The Omni-Star exited the Vortex at the Station-Keeping setting and came to a hover. She drifted slowly with the hundred-mile-wide transparent sphere-shaped city filling half the windshield. Zeta looked good, almost as if they had been gone for a long time. With all rotor pods reengaged, Sheldon began his approach for the second time and returned to his parking place.

The crew spent a few hours coming down off a high of the last eight-day experience. They were bright enough to understand just how beneficial and important the added capability would be. A capability that enables them to find their origin, however humble or exalted it may be; just so it's real. To voice the sentiment of the late Isaac Jacob Henson of Research One: "Mankind has a right to know the truth, whatever it is."

The next morning, following breakfast, it was back to the vigil of finding the source of the Moai's, and with it, it was believed, the giants', and man's, beginnings. The teams would be back to their task, pouring over records, looking for a clue as to where to begin a search. The historians on board were to begin a documentary-type tour of the spaceport, recording it for the peoples of earth.

Jimmy and Bruce were having breakfast with Mentar and Kronos. Jimmy brought up something that has been playing in his mind since the quest of the Moai's origin had become a solid cause. He looked up at Mentar and Kronos. "Mentar," he began, "some of you, your race, should be with us when we find the source, and I am saying *when*, because we are committed to this, the source of that sentient material that resulted in both of us. It obviously affects you as much as it does me. The difference in our respective sizes was the result of an outside influence, the sentience, the real us, is the same. The same."

Mentar was quiet for a moment, then looked at Jimmy and nodded. "I've been thinking about that too. I even thought about committing our ship to accompany you. However, we do not yet have the hull coating necessary for wormhole travel. But, I and a few of my crew, could join you on the Omni-Star for this historic journey. Kronos and my son are now experienced and capable of handling the affairs of Zannia during my absence."

Jimmy nodded. "That's what I would suggest. The Omni-Star has the modified accommodations for five of you. Mentar, I think it's really important that you and I be together for this."

With youthful excitement in his eyes, Mentar smiled, "I'll pick my team."

The science teams in the Library, Spaceport Zeta, began a daily vigil to find that clue....the birthplace of the Moai.

...AND THE JOURNEY CONTINUES!

DAN HOLT and MAX HOLT

ABOUT THE AUTHORS

Dan Holt is a U.S. Army veteran, having served three years as a Communications Specialist in Germany. He spent the remainder of his civilian career as a self-taught engineer, designing and testing large-scale production equipment for the file folder industry. The efficiency and durability of his designs even garnered interest from some foreign manufacturers.

In retirement, Dan has used his writing skills to express his continuing fascination with science fiction. His variety in sci-fi thought is evident in his other novels, SLEEP MODE and KEEPSAKE. The Underneath the Moon series, Sleep Mode and Keepsake are all now available on audio through www.audible.com. See all of Dan's books at the publisher's website, www.maxholtmedia.com.

Contact Dan through his Amazon Author's Page. https://www.amazon.com/Dan-Holt/e/B012LRN65K/ref=sr_ntt_srch_lnk_1?qid=1491 001715&sr=8-1

DAN HOLT and MAX HOLT

Max Holt is a retired U.S. Army pilot, having served 22 years on active duty, including two combat tours in Vietnam. He is an avid science fiction reader and writer. Max started his publishing company, Max Holt Media, in 2015. This book continues Max's partnership with his brother, Dan Holt, to write more of the UNDERNEATH THE MOON saga, expected to continue for several more volumes. They are also partnering in a new series, entitled...AI RISING. Book One...THE DOME, was released in 2017.

Max and his wife Sandy have two sons and six grandchildren. They enjoy traveling and have collected flags from 37 countries. Other than the USA, their favorites have been Switzerland, Austria, Italy and the UK, where they have established a life-long friendship with a family in Darlington, England. They now live in Mount Juliet, near Nashville, Tennessee.

Contact Max: www.maxholtmedia.com
               max@maxholtmedia.com
On Twitter - @maxholtmedia

Other Sci-Fi books by Max Holt:
   Alien Planet
Series – AI Rising (Book One) THE DOME, with
      Dan Holt

www.ingramcontent.com/pod-product-compliance
Lightning Source LLC
Chambersburg PA
CBHW061559170626
46811CB00001B/250